T0064616

Who Are We?

Mikaela A. McCoy

authorHOUSE®

AuthorHouse™
1663 Liberty Drive
Bloomington, IN 47403
www.authorhouse.com
Phone: 1 (800) 839-8640

Published by AuthorHouse   04/27/2015

ISBN: 978-1-5049-0872-6 (sc)
ISBN: 978-1-5049-0871-9 (e)

Print information available on the last page.

*Any people depicted in stock imagery provided by Thinkstock are
models, and such images are being used for illustrative purposes only.
Certain stock imagery © Thinkstock.*

This book is printed on acid-free paper.

*Because of the dynamic nature of the Internet, any web
addresses or links contained in this book may have changed
since publication and may no longer be valid. The views
expressed in this work are solely those of the author and do
not necessarily reflect the views of the publisher, and the
publisher hereby disclaims any responsibility for them.*

Chapter 1

I'm sitting on the ledge of the cliff, it's a secluded place in the woods a mile from my house. It's an area of Louisville where nobody comes unless you're a junkie, like me, or you're just looking for a good time, if you catch my drift.

I pull a cigarette from the almost empty pack and stick it between my lips, pull out my lighter, touch it to the cig and inhale deeply. It feels good to smoke. Letting the smoke consume me, like it's a part of me that I want to keep forever and never forget. Unlike my past. I look in the pack and realize I only have one left.

"Shit," I mumble under my breath. I pull my cigarette out of my mouth and exhale the smoke. A cool summer breeze blows through while the moon shines brightly, illuminating the night.

My mother is probably wondering where I am. She's always bugging me with the same questions: "Sheryl where have you been?" and "Are you still smoking Sheryl?" and "Why don't you make new friends?" By now she should make a recording so I can ignore it instead of her. It's a never ending cycle.

I take another long drag off my cigarette as the wind blows through my long black hair. It's not my natural color. I'm a natural brunette but I despise brown hair. Brown hair reminds me of Carla, brown hair to her ass. I like my black hair that falls just below my shoulder blades. My eyes are a blue green color like my dead beat fathers; and believe me if I could change my eye color I would at the drop of a hat. Frank left me and Carla when I was thirteen. He ran off with some stripper named Sugar Sparkle and never looked back. When dear old dad left I started doing drugs and drinking, and by fourteen or fifteen I began having sex. My mother thinks I'm still a virgin. I laugh a little at this. She is clueless as to everything I do except smoke. She can smell it on my breath and on my clothes. Most of the time I'm at a friend's house when I drink. That way she never knows I drink at all.

I quit doing drugs, however, because I hated the way they made me feel. Unlike most druggies, the high made me violent and angry instead of all happy and chill. Which there are only two people at Cliff Point who do drugs.

"You shouldn't be out here alone," a male voice says. "It gets pretty dangerous after dark Sheryl and you know that." His voice wraps around each word, its eerily soft.

"Yeah, well if anything happened to me you'd be to blame," I say and exhale a puff of smoke. "Carla would find you and turn you in." Carla being my mother's name. I haven't called her mom since I began drinking.

"That stingy bitch couldn't find me if she tried," he says in his deep voice. "I could run from here to Timbuktu and she'd never find me."

"Snake, she could if she tried. She'd pry it out of Wolf," I tell him. Snake is not his real name. His real name is Carlos. He got his name because he is a snake of a guy. He can play you in a heartbeat and leave you full of poison from his dirty ways. His brother, who we named Wolf, is a stingy little fucker. He is all bark and no bite. Ironic huh? He'll turn information on you in a heartbeat to make some fast cash.

"I could keep Wolf silent," he says, his lips pull into a salacious smile. Oh to know what he's thinking. Him and his evil thoughts. "Can I bum one?"

"Hell no, I've got one left until Carla gives me money from the child support," I tell him. He sighs heavily. "Shit, take it," I snap and throw him the pack. He laughs a little. Damn him, he knew I'd give it to him. I toss him the lighter since he never has one and put my cigarette out and stare into the dark oblivion beyond the cliff.

"You know we've been coming here for years and we're the only two who haven't fucked each other," Snake says with a sly smile. I smirk a little, then remember his ruthlessness after I fucked his brother. Constantly wanting in my pants, practically chasing me for sex.

"I don't give a shit, and we never will. You're like my brother Snake and so is Wolf even though he was my third," I admit. Wolf and I were drunk when we did it, I never really remembered what happened except I drank a lot and there was a lot of empty vodka and beer bottles in my bed the next morning.

He takes a long drag off the cigarette I gave him then tilts his head back and exhales making smoke rings in the air. "What number will I be?"

"Number never," I reply coldly.

"Ouch, that stings," he jokes.

"Oh whatever," I snap. I hop off the cliff and stand next to him. Snake stands at least a foot taller than me. He's eighteen and so am I. His black hair all tousled up from him running his fingers through it. I've seen him shirtless; he has a very nice body, but not my type. "I'll see ya' 'round Snake, gotta get home before Carla worries about where her 'precious baby girl is'," I say like my mom used to when I was little.

"Alright, hey thanks for the smoke," he hollers after me. He adds a wink and smirks at me.

"Yeah, yeah," I say. "Tell Wolf he's an ass for me alright? And tell Momma Jeanine I said hey," I add as I walk backwards away from him.

"Sure will," he replies. I watch him as he jumps over the cliff. It's not that far a drop, Snake is tall enough to hit the bottom and not injure himself.

I walk with my hands in my pockets. Damn Snake, taking my last smoke before my dad pays child support money. It's a good thing Carla found him. Without that money I wouldn't be able to smoke or drink. I kick at the rocks on the pavement, not giving a care in the world to the traffic passing me. Only thinking about me and the fact that I'll go insane without another smoke before Friday.

I call Snake's and Wolf's momma my mom. She understands me and gives me extra money if I need it to buy more smokes. I ran into Snake and Wolf my first time I went to Cliff Point. They took me in and have cared for me ever since. Momma Jeanine lets me stay over when Carla decides to mother me and discuss my wicked ways. Saying I have no friends and all. I do have friends. They're called Marlboro Reds, vodka, whiskey, and then there is Snake and Wolf and their momma. There is also everyone else at Cliff Point. Those are "friends" only called this because you need a stress reliever and they can make you forget it all in fifteen minutes.

I look up at the sky and notice the moon drifting away. I look at my phone and notice it's almost five AM. Carla is going to be pissed. Oh well. I walk in the front door and she's asleep on the couch. Papers scattered around her. Her usual. I quietly walk up the stairs to my room. I strip and stand in my bra and thong then climb into bed. I dropped out of high school my senior year. I can't stand stingy bitches who act fake all the time to impress their mommies and daddies. However, Carla wasn't too happy when I did drop out. I got the "You're going to be a stripper if you don't stay in school" speech when she found out.

I think everyone's parents have that speech saved for their daughters when they think about dropping out of school or do drop out of school. And if you haven't heard it, or a reference to it, here's the short version:

"You wanna drop out of high school? You do that and college is out the window! You can't get a job without a high school diploma. You can't get into college without a high school education. What about a GED? Yeah maybe college is possible then. But with no money you become a stripper, and then you're pole dancing and shanking your rump and your chest all over Vegas or the streets. Then you're even more broke only living on a few dollars. And that is what happens when you drop out."

Yes, that's the short version. May not seem short but there it is. And trust me the long version would take a while. Carla's took about three hours if I remember correctly.

A few hours of just me starring at the ceiling pass when my bed room door opens. Violently, I might add. Oh here we go. Carla the angry mom, always angry but I don't care. "Where have you been?" she questions. More like snaps.

"Out," I reply. Short and simple replies get nowhere but I hate talking to her. Talking to her is like talking to a brick wall.

"You have a curfew young lady," she tells me for the millionth time.

"Last I checked Carla I'm eighteen. A legal adult. I have no curfew," I spit at her. I get out of my bed and walk into the bathroom and slam the door shut. One day it'll get stuck and I'll be glad when it does. Then I can leave through the bathroom window and never have to open it to see her face on the other side.

"This conversation is not over Sheryl!" my mother shouts. She never swears. She hates those words. She used them with Frank only because he used them to hurt her, as she tells me. I wouldn't put hurting a woman passed Frank, he seems all the more capable of murdering someone.

"Fuck off," I yell back.

"Oh the language," I hear her mumble. "What have I done to make you this way? I've given you all you could ever want."

I walk out of the bathroom and stand in front of her with my toothbrush in my mouth. "Always up my ass. Telling me my father died in Afghanistan when he's not even part of the military. Lying to me is what made me this way," I snap at her. I turn back around and slam the door in her face. I hear her walk away and I open the bathroom door. I sigh with relief. I wish she would stay out of my life.

I shower then change into jeans and a tank top. My jeans are always skin tight as well as my tank tops or any clothing I wear. That's how any girl who goes to Cliff Point dresses. Tight clothing and sneakers. I walk out of my closet to see Snake sitting on my bed. "Nice thong," he smirks.

"Thanks," I say sarcastically. "One you'll never get into or get me out of."

"Here," he says and hands me a pack of Marlboro Reds. "Since I took ya last one last night. Momma bought you a whole pack. She said not to worry about paying her back."

"I'll thank her when I see her," I tell him.

He nods. "Carla seemed pissed this morning."

"Always is when I don't come home when she wants," I explain. "You know that Snake."

"Yeah, well," he shrugs and glances around my unkempt room. "Anyway, all of us are gonna chill at Cliff Point. Word around says Isaiah will be there." His eyes glaze over as he says Isaiah's name. He knows I always slept with Isaiah. Isaiah has a lot to offer a girl.

"Oh yeah? Well he better be," I smirk. "I've missed him at Cliff Point." *Missed is an understatement!* My mind yells at me. I shrug off my internal outburst and focus on the here and now. After all Snake is in my bedroom.

"I bet you have," he smirks. I shove him playfully. "He makes you scream and howl like a wolf when you sleep with him," he adds and leans back acting like he's howling.

"Awe is someone upset because he can't get in my pants?" I tease. Snake has been trying for years and still hasn't succeeded.

"Sheryl I'm the only guy you haven't slept with at Cliff Point," he says. "You've gone through all the guys. Even the new guys but not me. Why is that?" he asks.

"Snake, you found me and took me in. How can I sleep with you knowing you saved me?" I question. "And I've only slept with Isaiah for the last year."

He rubs the back of his neck in exasperation. His hair falls in his eyes and he looks damn sexy like that. "If that's why you won't sleep with me it has got to be something else," he snarls. "I see how ya stare at me sometimes. And even some of the guys know you want a piece of this. It's obvious Sheryl."

"Damn it Snake!" I yell. "If I ever wanted to sleep with you I would have done it by now," I hiss.

He huffs and lights up a cigarette. "I'll see you at Cliff Point tonight then," he says. He climbs out of my window and holds onto the edge. "In Isaiah's car," he winks. I throw a shoe at him and miss as he jumps away from the window. "I'll keep this until I see you tonight!" he hollers up at me.

Damn he's got my good sneaker too. "Snake give that back!" but he's out of ear shot and can't hear me. Oh well, I'll get it back. In the meantime I'll pay a visit to Momma Jeanine. Make him give me my sneaker back when I get there.

I walk to Snakes house and see her sitting on the porch. "Sheryl baby is that you?" she asks.

"Yeah momma it's me," I smile. "Thanks for the smokes," I tell her.

"Well Snake told me he took ya last one so I figure I go buy you some more since you's waiting on the child support payment from ya daddy," she says.

"Yeah, he ain't payin' up any time soon. He's always late," I explain with a crooked grin. She pats my shoulder. "Is Snake or Wolf around? Or maybe both?" I ask her.

"Both of 'em is out back messin' with that old car," she tells me. I nod and walk around back. She hates that they always work the car but she always says it's better they're doing something productive instead of sitting on their asses all day.

"Snake!" I yell.

"Dammit!" he yells as he hits his head on the hood. "What the hell you want?" he asks pointing a wrench at me.

"My shoe back, it's my good sneaker."

"Oh you mean this one?" Wolf holds it in the air. Huge, sly grin plastered on his oil covered face.

"Yeah that one," I say and snatch it from him. I slip it on my barefoot and lace it up. "What time we meetin' at Cliff Point?" I ask them.

"Oh yeah, word around says Isaiah will be there," Wolf beams at me. I flip him off, he grins wildly and continues. "Meet up at dusk," he tells me.

"I'll be there," I say and walk off.

"Is that all ya came for?" Wolf shouts.

"Yeah, that and to thank Momma for the smokes," I reply. Both of them shake their heads and laugh. Out of all of the kids at Cliff Point I'm the only one with manners. I thank Momma Jeanine again and head back up the dirt road to the main highway to head back home until dusk.

Carla isn't home when I get there. She's probably at work like always. I eat whatever I can find and then watch some TV. My phone buzzes. "You comin' to Cliff Point?" it's Isaiah.

"I'm always there. You however lack presence when I need to forget" I send back.

"Not my fault," he sends me. I huff.

"You comin'?" I ask him.

"I'll be there. Meet me at my car once you get there. I'll show you a good time," he says. I smirk. It's about time he showed.

Cliff Point is about the only place for people like us to hang out. This college town is too much for us so we go there to get away from all the rich college kids. They don't bother us so we don't bother them. It's as simple as that.

Around six o'clock I start walking toward Cliff Point. I pull out a cigarette and light it up on the way there. Smoking brings me relief to an extent. Isaiah on the other hand makes me forget. I've slept with all the guys, old and new, at Cliff Point but none compare to Isaiah. Not even in the slightest. I smirk at my thoughts and grin like a loon. *You know you feel for him! Don't hide it!* I frown at my internal self. I do not feel for Isaiah, sexually maybe, but nothing more. *Stop lying to yourself! Don't hide the feelings!*

I stomp the ground and shout, "Shut up! Shut up! Shut up!" Stupid internal battles. I know what I feel but I'm not feeling that towards Isaiah. I throw my cigarette to the ground. I look up at the fading daylight and close my eyes. "Just another night, doing the same thing. The normal," I remind myself. *Whatever, keep lying to yourself.* I shrug.

I have a half a mile left to go until I reach Cliff Point. I see my mother's car heading toward me. She slows and then stops in front of me. "Sheryl do not go to that place!" she yells. "Get in this car right now!"

I step over to her car, "ya know Carla, I'm eighteen. I can do whatever the hell I want to. And I'm going whether you like it or not," I tell her with an attitude. I back away from her car and she stares at me. "You gonna go or you just gonna sit there all night?" I ask and point towards home.

"I understand you are an adult but you will do as I say as long as you live under my roof you hear me?" she scowls.

"Yeah, yeah," I say. "I'll have my shit out tonight when I get home later," I snap and walk away from her car. I light up another cigarette and hear her drive off. I turn around to see her top a hill then she's gone. "Thank you," I sigh. She frustrates me so much.

I continue to walk. Damn her and her rules. "My house my rules Sheryl," she tells me all the time. I hate her. She despises me and asks me all the time why I am the way I am. I've explained why and she still doesn't understand. I see a group of other people who walk to Cliff Point. Three of which are guys whom I've slept with. The other two are girls. Poor girls, I've never seen them and if they're sleeping with those guys, ha they will not enjoy it.

I pass them and they all call my name. "Sheryl!"

"What?" I snap.

"Isaiah's waitn' for ya," they all say. "Gonna howl all night long!" And he should be. When he's at Cliff Point he only sleeps with me.

"Yeah, yeah. I know," I reply and keep walking. *Tell him! Tonight!* I shrug off the thoughts and keep walking towards the cliff.

It's almost dark out. Dusk will soon fade. I reach Cliff Point and see Snake and Wolf standing with three other guys. I walk over to them. "Seen Isaiah yet?" I ask them.

"Oh yeah, I did notice him pull in," Jack grins. "Let's hear that howl Sheryl. We will be soon." He winks and sips his beer.

"He's waitn' by his car for ya," Wolf tells me. I look around them to see Isaiah staring at me from across the way. He pulls the cigarette from his lips and exhales. Damn he's so hot.

"He's been waitin' a while. Maybe thirty minutes," Snake adds. "Keep him waitin' too long and he might fuck someone else."

"Very doubtful Snake. You're just saying that 'cause you want me to sleep with you," I sneer at him. "But thanks Wolf," I reply and walk towards Isaiah's car.

As I walk across the flat terrain of the cliff, I notice all the people hooking up for the night. All stop to stare at me as I walk towards Isaiah. They all know what's about to happen. They all listen. Some stop hooking up just to listen to me howl. Everyone gets a kick out of hearing me. Snake, however does not. He'd rather be fucking some girl or drowning it out with his music.

Isaiah smirks as he sees me. He runs a hand through his hair and winks. *You know what you feel! Tell the guy!* I burry the thought deep into my brain and continue to walk to Isaiah. He steps away from his car a few feet and crosses his arms so they flex. It makes my insides tremble.

I reach him and he pulls me close. "I thought you weren't gonna show," he says in his deep voice. He's taller than me with jet black hair and molten gray eyes. He toss's his cigarette and squeezes my ass. "Still firm I see, I've missed that ass of yours," he whispers seductively in my ear. He leans down and kisses my neck.

"Oh Isaiah," I moan. "It's been a while," I say. He nibbles my neck up to my ear lobe then bites it and tugs. I melt and moan again.

"Hush, don't make any noise until you are in my car," he orders. I comply and nod. "What do you say?" he asks me.

"Yes sir," I reply. My blood is thick and heavy. My muscles clench as he kisses my neck again.

"I don't think you need this," he says and pushes my denim jacket off to reveal my tank top. "Or those take them off," he says talking about my shoes. I take them off and he puts them in his trunk. "Now, you know what to do," he says. I nod and he opens the car door. I crawl to the back seat and lay across it. He climbs in and gets on top of me. "You know what these jeans do to me," he snarls.

"It's the only reason I wore them," I reply. He growls low in his throat and proceeds to kiss my lips. I fist my hands in his hair and tug. He moans into my mouth. I feel his bulge at my pelvic bone. He pulls my tank top off and then my bra. He starts to toy with me.

Soon he is pulling my jeans off. "Always wearing the outfits that drive me crazy," he says. I smirk up at him. He starts kissing my lips again and I work his shirt up and off of him. I work on his jeans next. Then his boxers. I've missed him touching me this way. He springs free and he rolls a condom on. He pulls my thong off and hovers over me.

"Take me," I moan as he kisses my chest. "Make me forget."

He slides into me and I moan loudly. "Let me hear you baby," he says then kisses my chest some more. He gently moves in and out of me. Back and forth in a slow motion.

"Harder Isaiah," I moan. He begins to move, really move. Thrusting into me faster and harder. I moan louder and louder. I feel my body build as he thrusts into me. His lips find mine and he kisses me.

"Mmm Sheryl," he moans. "You do things to me."

I just moan in response. He does things to me that I can't explain. *You need to tell him! Tell him now!* I ignore my thoughts and focus on the fact that tonight is a normal night between me and Isaiah.

Hands are everywhere. All touch and sensation. I wrap my legs around him, pulling him closer to me. My hands go to his back and I scratch him. He moans loudly in response. He kisses my neck and I fist one hand in his hair. I can feel both of us coming close. Oh so close. Isaiah moves fast. I can feel his muscles tense up. My body building further and further. I'm so close…

"Come for me baby," he growls and I do as if on command and shout his name loudly. I claw at his back and scratch. I feel his body go ridged and he collapses on top of me. He looks up at me and kisses me gently then eases out of me. He puts a cigarette in his mouth and lights it then hands it to me. I take a long drag off it then hand it back. I exhale and smoke fills the car.

"Like old times," I say.

"Like old times for sure," he says and hands me the cigarette back. He toss's me my clothes and I slip them on. He does the same and dresses himself. "Life is like sex ya know?" he says and throws something out the window.

"How so?" I ask him.

He takes the cigarette from me and inhales. He exhales then continues. "People help you undress but once you've been fucked you get dressed alone. Life is the same way. People help you out until you fuck up then you're all alone," he explains.

"Very true," I reply. He nods. "Thank you for that. I needed that," I tell him.

"That's what I'm for," he smirks.

He always has a way with me that makes me want him more. After I slept with Isaiah the first time I never slept with anyone else. Only him. And he knows that. *Tell him! He needs to know! Its quiet, just tell him!* I shake my head at my internal battle with my "feelings" for Isaiah. I'll never win it over, but it's best to ignore it for now.

We sit there silent for a while until Isaiah looks at me. It's a strange look. One I've never seen him use before. He tosses the cigarette butt out the window then rolls the window up. "Sheryl we've been sleeping together for a long time," he tells me. He says it softly. Isaiah, soft? He looks at me with gentle eyes. Two things Isaiah never does.

"A year," I reply cautiously. Afraid of what he's going to say or do. *He has the feeling! He's going to tell you how he feels! And you feel the same! You must say it! You must!* Oh shut it internal voice. I'm not saying how I feel.

"Yeah," he says. "And just like you I haven't slept with anyone else. You are the only girl I've slept with since I first slept with you," he tells me. Where is he going with this? "I can't eat or sleep or think or do anything without thinking about you."

Now's your time! Sheryl tell him you love him. You know you do! Ugh! Okay fine I do love him. I've always felt this way for him but it could never work between us at Cliff Point.

"Isaiah what are you trying to say?" I ask him. Panic starts ripping through me. What he's about to say is impossible. It can't happen between us. Not now, not ever. *Stop lying to yourself! It is possible Sheryl!*

He sighs a heavy sigh then grabs my hands. He looks into my eyes, his face very serious and his grey eyes are as gentle as a lamb. Then he opens his mouth and says what my internal voice has been saying for the past fifteen minutes. "Sheryl, I think I'm in love with you."

Chapter 2

I told you so! I told you so! I shake my head at my internal self. I look at Isaiah in shock. Nobody at Cliff Point dates anyone from Cliff Point. It's not possible. I scratch my head while he looks at me. "Sheryl say something," he wills me. "Please."

"Isaiah nobody from Cliff Point dates," I tell him. "It's weird and unheard of. How do you think we could get away with dating around here huh?" My internal self shakes her head and sighs.

"We could date in secret," he suggests. "Nobody would have to find out. Just me and you would know. Please Sheryl. You are all I think about. Night and day. And when you hadn't gotten here, I was gonna find you because I think I'm falling in love with you."

"Stop saying it!" I lean forward and put my head in my hands and think for a minute. *No need to think! You love the boy! He loves you! Don't overthink anything.* "What do I need to do when I get out of the car?" I ask him. And yet again my internal battle with my love for Isaiah is silenced and put away.

"Act like you normally do when you get out of my car. Satisfied and sore," he tells me. I nod and he looks at me. "Please give us a try. If you don't like it we can end it."

"Isaiah let me think on it for a few days and then I'll get in touch with you somehow," I tell him. "But until then I need some time. I'm leaving Carla's house tonight. Going somewhere, I don't know where. Just let me think on it." *Stop thinking and just tell him!*

"Alright," he says softly. "Now get out of the car like nothing happened except a good time," he orders me. And back to his normal self. Why is he so…so…I don't know? Confusing? Maybe, but Isaiah is Isaiah. With him, it's either take it or leave it. No in between with him. Which is probably why I'm in love with him. *Yes! I win this round! You love him! Now just tell him Sheryl!*

I get out of the car and make my way to the trunk and retrieve my shoes and jacket. Isaiah pulls me to him one more time and whispers something in my ear. "I'll be waiting for an answer." He holds me at arm's length and he looks stern, he nods and mouths okay. I just nod and walk back towards Snake and Wolf. I get to them and pull a smoke out and light it.

"Have a good time?" Snake laughs as he sips a beer.

"Sounds like you did," Jack says and makes a howling motion. "Man, we thought you to would go on all night long."

"Always do with Isaiah," I smile. I grab the beer from Snake and turn it up. "We got anything stronger?" I ask. Wolf hands me a bottle of vodka and I smile even bigger. "Just what I need," I murmur as I turn the bottle up. I notice Isaiah watching me intently from his car. Was he serious about us dating? Or was I hallucinating?

I don't know. *You know he is! Stop thinking and just agree already!*

"Earth to Sheryl," Snake says as he waves a hand in front of my face. "If you're gonna move out of Carla's you better get on it. It's nearing four in the morning."

"Alright, I'll see you guys later," I say and walk off. Wolf goes to take the vodka from me but I hold it to me. "Get your own damn bottle of vodka," I snarl. He retreats his hand and backs off. That's what I thought. He knows I'll hit him hard enough to keep him on the ground long enough to sleep on it.

I walk along the road taking swigs of vodka here and there. Kicking rocks and pebbles as I go. Not too far to Carla's but far enough for me to be completely wasted by the time I get there. Hopefully she'll be asleep. I pull out a cigarette and light it. I exhale the smoke in a large cloud around me. I feel great. Free actually if you could call it that. All that matters is that I'm walking to Carla's to retrieve my belongings and live elsewhere. I feel fuzzy headed and my vision is blurry but I've walked this path drunk so many times I know where I'm going.

Don't forget Isaiahs confession! Now it's your turn to confess! You have to do it Sheryl sooner rather than later! "Oh shut it internal battle, I'm too wasted for this shit right now," I say out loud as I walk. Oh great, and now I'm replying to myself. Someone will think I'm insane and throw me in the looney bin for talking and answering myself.

I hear a car at least a half mile behind me. I dismiss it. I feel the urge to vomit. I drop the bottle in my hand and fall to my knees and hurl all over the side of the road. I feel like its burning my throat. Which it probably is, it's all alcohol. "Damn Sheryl how much of that did you drink?" I hear someone ask. It's only then do I notice that car was closer than I thought and that Isaiah was following me home.

I hold up the half empty bottle for him to see. I wipe my face off with my hand and stand. "Why you following me huh?" I snarl at him. *He loves you! He's making sure you get home safe Sheryl. Jeez use your head! Oh right, being hammered prevents that.* I snarl at my internal battle.

"I um..." he stops and I cover my mouth and turn away from him. I vomit again. Usually I can keep it down. But I guess I drank more than I thought. "You need a ride home?" he asks me.

"I can walk, it's only a half mile left to go," I snap at him. *Stop being so cold and go! Oh and tell him you love him so the battle is won internally again!* Will this ever stop? I sigh, I guess it won't as long as I keep battling myself about things like this.

"Sheryl you are in a drunken stooper throwing your guts up on the side of the highway. Let me take you home." Isaiah is not one to argue with. I step towards him and trip over my feet. He catches me before I fall. "Easy," he whispers. He helps me in his car then he drives off.

Isaiah drives slow down the road to keep me from puking in his car. His car is his baby. You don't fuck with him or his car. He stops the car outside Carla's house. I look at my phone. Fuck! It's almost five AM. I open the door and get out of his car. "Hey," he hollers.

"What?" I snap back.

"Don't forget to think on it," he replies.

I nod and unlock the front door. I hear Isaiah's car drive away and I sigh when I open the door. Carla's asleep on the couch as usual. I walk, more like stomp, up the stairs to my room. I get in the shower and hurl again. When I get out I change into jeans and tank top and get all my shit together. I've got to get out of here. It does me no good to sit in this hell hole with Carla. My phone rings and I answer it. "What Snake?" I growl at him.

"I'm waiting for ya. Momma said you can stay with us," he tells me. I smile at his response. "Now hurry before Carla wakes up."

"Yeah, yeah, I'm comin'," I tell him. "Meet me by my window."

"Already here," he says. I hang up the phone and open the window. I throw as much of my stuff out that I want and jump down. "Nice to see your hung-over self," he grins.

"Fuck off, I drank more than I thought I did," I hiss. *Little love drunk maybe?* My internal self laughs at me.

"Sure," he laughs. I shove him and he picks up my things. "Oh Momma has a surprise for ya. Well more like me, Wolf, and Momma."

I nod and we make the long walk to his house. Snake has a car but prefers to walk unless it's too far to walk. Which is probably why he's got such a nice body. That and he works on lots of cars, hefting around heavy parts to fix them and sell them.

Along the way I think of what Isaiah told me. He loves me. I wonder if I should tell someone. *Yes! Tell Isaiah you love him!* No. We said we would keep it a secret. Ugh! He is so frustrating. I kick at the dirt on the dirt road to Snakes place. I hate having internal battles with myself. I always lose. That's one of my flaws. My internal battles lead me to telling someone. Then everyone finds out. But nobody from Cliff Point can find out about this. Nobody. But that's only if I agree to it.

"Internal argument again?" Snake asks me.

"Yeah," I reply and kick a rock down the street.

"Who's winning? You are the internal battle?" he asks me. And before I can answer her speaks again. "I bet it's the internal battle by the way you're sighin' and kickin' rocks down the street."

"Internal battle is winning, yes," I snap at him. *Only because you are believing what I've been saying for the last six months!* "But not for long."

"Ya know ya wanna tell me," he grins and nudges me.

"I can't Snake, not this time," I tell him. Which I can't. Really can't. His violent nature is why. He has a rap sheet a mile long in the violence department

"Sheryl I'll get it out of ya some way, somehow," he smirks at me. "I always do," he adds and starts walking backwards in front of me.

"Nope, not this time." He just laughs and continues to walk backwards. "Would you turn around? Ya makin' me nervous. Ya gonna walk into something."

"Nah, I'll be good. Walked this path a million times."

After ten minutes he turns back around and we continue walking, silently to his house. We both turn down the dirt road to his place. Back off in the woods. Momma Jeanine likes her hidden spaces. That's why she doesn't object to us going to Cliff Point. She went there when she was our age. It's off in the woods. Secluded. The way Momma Jeanine likes it.

Momma Jeannine keeps to herself. Doesn't bother others or get wrapped up in any drama. Yeah she fixes problems for me and her boys but that's about it. She's content in her own way. When her husband, John, passed a few years ago she started doin' more for herself. Snake and Wolf are grown so she leaves them to themselves.

"Sheryl, baby nice to see ya," Momma Jeanine says as she hugs me. "I gotcha room all set. Then go out back with Snake and Wolf. They gotcha a surprise," she tells me.

"Alright, thanks Momma," I smile. She smiles and nods. Snake's place isn't much but it's like my home. The furniture is as new as you want it to be. Most of it is new but the rest is rotting away. Much like the trailer they live in. This place is closer to Cliff Point than Carla's. Less than half a mile. I follow Snake out back and he stops me and covers my eyes. "Snake what the hell are you doing?" I ask him and try to twist out of his hold.

"So you can't see the surprise," he tells me. I huff and he uncovers my eyes. "This is yours," he says and dangles the keys in front of my face.

My face lights up and I gasp. He drops the keys into my hands and I walk towards it. I run my fingers along the smooth black paint. "You're giving me your'86 Camaro?" I ask him.

"That's why I've been fixing it up. You got a license but no car," he says. "I've got one and so does Wolf. This one's yours."

"Thanks you guys," I say. "Can I drive it?" *Well you better! Look at it! And yours!*

"Yeah it's yours," Wolf says. I get in the driver's seat and start the car.

The way the engine rumbles ignites my blood and sends tingles through my body. I feel it in my bones. It's like I'm waking up for the first time. I'm behind the wheel of a beast of a motor.

I take it out on the open road and let lose. I press the gas to the floor and drive. A smile plays on my lips. This is the best day of my life. I shriek with excitement as I drive down the highway. *This is freedom! Freedom at its finest Sheryl!*

I turn around and drive back to Snakes and smile the whole way back. Having a car is the best feeling in the world. Carla refused to get me one because she was always afraid I would leave. Well, at the time, I didn't have a car and I still left her house. I'm eighteen so I can do what I want anyway.

I park the car next to Snake's and get out with a smile on my face. "You like?" Momma Jeanine asks me.

"Very much so," I tell her, a wicked grin plastered on my face.

"I'm glad," she says. "Snake'll buy the gas for it. I'll buy ya smokes. We gotcha covered Sheryl," she explains.

"Thanks Momma," I say and hug her. I only hug a few people and Momma Jeanine is one of those people. I walk inside and sit on the couch. It's got missed-matched cushions but it's comfy. Snake plops down beside me and grins. "What?" I ask.

"Me and Wolf came up with a nickname for ya," he tells me.

"Oh shit, what is it?" I ask him. They have come up with four other nicknames for me in the past. None of which worked or stuck for that matter. I just laugh at his attempts on nicknames for me. They have tried Black, Moon, Midnight, and Jet. Black because I went through a phase where I wore only black clothes. *It was more like a Goth phase gone horribly wrong!* I scowl at my internal self again.

Moon because I howled at the moon when I slept with someone. *Which would have worked if you were still sleeping with everyone and not just Isaiah.* I sigh, Isaiah made me feel different. *You fell in love with him! Which brings us back to-* no not right now internal self.

Midnight because I usually only go to Cliff Point at midnight. *When you don't sleep at night. Or if it's a Monday night when no one is there at all.* I only go alone unless it's a meet night. And then Jet because Snake said I had a fascination with flying. Which I do not. Planes horrify me. *He was messing with you! He knows you hate planes!*

"Viper," he says.

"Why?" I ask him.

"Because you leave a poisonous bite behind anywhere you go," he explains.

"No," I scoff. *What is he completely dimwitted?!*

"And why not?" he asks. "You come up with one then. You never like our ideas. And besides me and Wolf seem to do all the nickname work anyway!"

"That nickname doesn't fit me," I tell him. "I want a badass name. One that makes people shiver when they hear it," I explain.

"Okay," he says. He sits there for a few minutes and thinks. He nods his head side to side. He always does that before he finally says something. "Why don't we just name you bad ass?" he smirks.

"No," I shove him. "Come on just think of one. It can't be that hard. We came up with Wolf's nickname in ten minutes. Mine is taking years. Just think of one."

"Only because Wolf is easy to name. Why do you think Momma named him Josh when he was born?" he asks me. We both laugh and sit in silence for a while and think. "Claw," he says eventually and grins at me.

"Claw?" I question. "What's the reason?" I ask him.

"Claw," he repeats. "Because you have sharp ass nails on those fingers. You could claw someone up if they mess with you," he explains. "Wolf has the mark to prove it too."

"Yeah, it fits her. Let's go with that," Wolf says. "My scars are faint but they're still there. And I don't want more."

Snake and I laugh. We both remember when I gave him those scars. It was a very satisfying day on my part. *Sure it was! It was also a month after you started falling or Isaiah!*

I think about the name and toss it around my head. Claw. That could work. And I could claw someone up with my nails. I look at my fingers. Sharp ass nails on my fingers. Yeah I like that name. "Claw it is then." Snake and Wolf grin and I just shake my head at them.

Chapter 3

Isaiah texts me, "meet at Cliff Point in an hour."

"In the middle of the day?"

"Yes."

"Fine." It's been four days since he told me he loves me. *Stop denying it! You love him too!* I frown at my internal battle. Nagging bitch.

I have done nothing but think about it. There is no harm in trying a relationship but it'd be weird. People who hang out at Cliff Point don't date others who hang out at Cliff Point. I mean there is one couple who is dating. Logan and Roxy have been the only people to date from Cliff Point. Both hang out at Cliff Point and they've been dating for four years. But they are the only couple from Cliff Point to date. They also started dating before they got there. Always hanging on each other, showing their affection for each other. It's sick, really.

Stop that! You know you would do that with Isaiah in a heat beat if you could tell someone you two are dating. "Would you top that?" I say to my internal battle. Besides, me and Isaiah aren't even dating. Yet.

Everyone has been calling me Claw. This nickname finally stuck. *It's about time a nickname stuck. Took long enough.* I snarl at my internal battle and she snarls back. I went to Cliff Point with Snake and Wolf and now everybody knows. It fits too. Two new guys showed last night and grabbed at me. I clawed their faces and now I have a story to back my new nickname.

Carla called me and begged me to come back home. My last check from my father came. I went and picked it up when she wasn't home. She cashed it and left it for me to retrieve. The last check is always the biggest. Forty grand. I counted it twice to make sure I had it all before I left Carla's. I got all forty grand. She agreed when we started getting them that I could have the money. She didn't need it. And why should she? She's a nurse. She makes plenty of money to support herself. I'm just glad I got the child support check.

Honestly I didn't think Carla would let me have it. During the trial, she acted like she would get it all and I would never see a dime. However, when we got home she told me I would get it all. Every penny. When she said this, I smiled from ear to ear and a few weeks later she handed me the first check. Well cash really, and I've been saving it since then. That was four years ago. Almost to the day.

I drive to the old country store to get more smokes. Big Red, the owner, knows me well and has them sitting on the counter when I get there. I hand him the money and he gives me a bottle of vodka. Which it's hiding in my car. If I don't hide it Snake and Wolf will drink it all. Big Red knows us all from the cliff. He's always got an eye and ear out for us if we need help.

Except Isaiah! "Oh shut it bitch," I whisper. Big Red hates Isaiah, for the sole reason that he slept with Isaiah's mother. Isaiah, according to rumors, threatened to kill him if he didn't leave his home. After that, the two have never crossed paths. One reason people cannot find out if Isaiah and I date.

I throw on some shoes and make my way out of the house. "Where are you going Claw?" Snake asks as I walk to my car. He's all curious and wanting answers.

"Out. And why does it matter to you?" I snap back.

"It doesn't, just curious," he replies. He grips the support beam on the porch and pulls himself up. He's always trying to impress me.

"Curious as ever, I'm afraid," I quip. "And stop with trying to impress me all the time. It's not gonna make me sleep with you."

"I know ya want all this!" he hollers at me and runs his hand over his body in a sexual manner.

I wave him off and get in my car and drive down to Cliff Point. It sucks that Snakes place is so far from the cliff. But I'm never in a hurry. Well maybe today, because I'm going to see Isaiah. I smile on the inside. *And make that a win for me again Sheryl!* I growl at her, I hate my internal battle wining.

I'm a few minutes late but it'll be alright. I see Isaiah leaning against his car. Jet black hair gleaming in the sun. Black shirt pulling and stretching around his muscular arms and chest. I turn my car off and open the door. The dust disappears and I close the door and lean against it.

"I thought you weren't gonna show," he says. A slight hint of worry etched on his face. Or is it fear? I don't know. "Nice car."

"I always show sooner or later," I sneer. I take a drag off my smoke then exhale before I speak again. "Thanks. Snake fixed her up for me."

"Isn't that nice," he says sarcastically. I smirk. "Word around says you've got a new name."

"That's right, and a story to back it." *Here we go, brag as usual.*

"Do tell," he smiles. His smile is perfect. It makes me melt.

My internal battle giggles and smiles. She's winning. Again.

I take my denim jacket off and toss it in my car. I know what my outfits do to him. I walk over to the cliff and sit on the edge. "Snake came up with it," I start. "Last night two new guys grabbed at me so I clawed both of them. Left claw marks on their faces." I inhale off my cigarette then exhale slowly. I feel him behind me. His arms wrap around me and he rests his chin on my shoulder. "I am no longer Sheryl," I tell him. "The names Claw." He laughs slightly at this. "What's so damn funny?" I snap.

"Badass name for a badass girl," he grins. "I like it. I'm glad you showed those two guys whose boss."

"Yeah? And what would you have done about it?" I ask him.

"Beat their asses for touching what's mine," he says and pinches my ass. "You know that no one touches what's mine."

"Ouch!" I squeal. "Last I checked I hadn't agreed to anything," I remind him. *You have agreed you just won't voice it!* Yeah 'cause you'll win again. That's why.

"I wish you would though," he whispers. "It's killin' me Claw, I need to know. Please. I just need a yes or no. it would make my life a hell of a lot easier if you would just answer me."

"Isaiah, there is only one couple here. Both from Cliff Point. Yeah they've been together four years but you only come round so little," I explain. "Even if we date in secret, when would I ever actually see you?"

"I've been coming back more in the past six months than I ever have. Think back," he tells me.

I think back over the past six months. I've spent most of my time here. Either during the day or at night, I'm almost always here. I think about just sitting here on the cliff. I always noticed a car but I thought it just appeared and somebody left it. I thought it was just here. I didn't think anyone was in it or owned it. The windows were too tinted for me to see inside it. I remember coming at night and seeing a shadow figure in the trees. Or hearing twigs snap or gravel crush under some ones feet. Lots of people come to Cliff Point alone, but when I came, I always thought I was alone. Nobody was here but me.

"That was you?" I question. "Watching me from the shadows? Stalking me because you love me?"

"Yeah, that was me. I watched you every time you came here. I watched as you smoked the night away or talked with Snake. I watched you drink and pass out later. All because of what I feel for you," he explains. "The nights I watched you talk with Snake was like a dagger twisting in my chest. I thought you and him were hooking up.

"Every time he touched you, you pushed away and I got a little more hopeful. The other night when you were out here, and Snake said you shouldn't be out here alone, I almost laughed at him. You've never been out here alone. Well for the past six months anyway."

"Then why approach me now? Why not approach me sooner?" I quiz him. My internal battle shakes her head at me and I scowl at her.

"I wanted to be sure I felt that way towards you," he replies softly. "And when you showed that night and I saw you walking towards me, I knew. I had known when I asked if you were coming here that night."

Isaiah has always been the type to just sleep around with girls. He never wanted a relationship with a girl before so if he wants one now, he's not lying about it. *Of course he is and so are you! Oh and looks as if*

I'm winning again! I ignore my internal battle and pull another cigarette out and light it. "Isaiah," I start then exhale. "Snake wants to sleep with me." I let it set in for a minute. "He can't figure out why I won't."

His grip on me tightens, "what do you tell him?" he asks me. His voice rising just enough to reveal his jealousy.

"That he's my brother and he saved me. It'd be too weird," I reply. "Yeah I slept with Wolf but that was a long time ago."

"He wants in your pants like his brother," he replies. "I remember a night when Wolf tried again." I laugh a little, as does Isaiah.

I nod, "well he's not going to get in my pants. I haven't slept with anyone but you since the first time we slept together."

"Me either," her replies.

I look out over the cliff towards the woods. "Sometimes I wish I could really forget it all. My dad, my mom, and all the lies between them." I put my cigarette out and look at Isaiah. He's looking up at me.

"I can help you forget," he smirks.

"Yeah, yeah, keep your pants on," I smile. I look back out over the cliff and breathe in deep. I look at my phone. It's almost four. Momma Jeanine will have dinner ready soon. "I gotta go. Momma Jeanine will worry if I'm not back before dinner."

"You stayin' at Snake's place?" he asks me.

"Yeah, I moved out of Carla's. That stingy bitch thought she could control me. I'm almost nineteen. I left and she can deal."

"Just be careful around him," he warns me. I nod. I walk over to my car and open the door. Isaiah shuts it and puts his hands on either side of me. "It's been four days Claw," he says. "I need an answer." His face inches from mine. Our lips centimeters apart. "Please give me an answer," he begs. "Please."

You're killing the boy! Do something to put him out of his misery please!

I look into his gray eyes and see nothing but promise. Slowly, I wrap my arms around his neck and press my lips to his. He moves his hands off my car to the sides of my face.

"How's that for an answer?' I ask him when I pull away.

"So it's a yes then?" he asks.

"Oh for the love of God, yes Isaiah," I tell him. "It is a yes," I repeat. *Ha! I win again! Two points for the internal battle!*

He smiles and the smile reaches his gray eyes. He kisses me once more then releases me. I open my car door then turn to face him. "Nobody can find out about us," he warns me.

"If Snake finds out he'd kill me and you," I reply. "Snake is over protective of me. Always has been and always will be."

"Yeah I know he is," Isaiah says. "When can I see you again?" he asks with a hopeful smile.

"Soon," is all I tell him. I get in my car and drive off. I look in the rear view mirror to see him getting in his car. God he's hot. And I am all his. Nobody messes with Isaiah's property. Which I can handle situations on my own. I clawed two guys last night. I've brawled with plenty of guys at Cliff Point. Nobody messes with me. Unless they are new guys. Then they fight me once and realize it's in their best interest to not even look at me wrong.

I reach Snake's place and get out of my car. I smell ribs smoking on the grill on the front porch. Momma Jeanine sure knows how to cook. Unlike Carla. It's always frozen TV dinners because Carla can't cook. Not even during the holidays. It was always pre-cooked meals. So I always came here for the holidays. Good home cooked food three times a day every day, it's nice. Especially during Christmas.

"I was beginnin' to worry about ya," Momma Jeanine says as I walk on the porch. "Tell momma where ya been."

"Cliff Point," I tell her. She just nods. She knows what we do there so she doesn't question it. Carla always does.

"Snake and Wolf's out back messin' with Roxy," she says. "Dinner will be ready in an hour or so," she adds.

"Alright," I say. I throw my denim jacket on my bed then head out back. "You two make that dog meaner than she's supposed to be," I tease.

"Hell, she only likes you and Momma," Snake replies. Roxy sees me and runs over to me. She's a hundred fifty pound Rottweiler. She's gray in the face but she can bite the shit out of you in a heartbeat. "See what I mean?" Snake says.

"I can't help that. I don't torment her," I tell him. I kneel down and pet her and she licks my face. "Isn't that right? Those two are mean. Sick'em!" I say.

Roxy growls and barks and lunges at Snake. He jumps up on the fence so she can't reach him. "Damn you Claw!" he hollers.

She lunges for Wolf next. He does the same as Snake and flips me off. "Fuck you Claw!" he shouts at me.

"You already have!" I holler back. He gasps then loses his balance and falls off the fence. Me and Snake bust out laughing. "Roxy come here girl!" I holler. She trots over to me and sits down. I pet her head then walk inside. Momma Jeanine stares at me. "Don't ask," I laugh.

"Wasn't gonna when it comes to you three," she says. "Tell them to wash up, dinner is finished and getting cold."

I nod and walk out back. "Momma says wash up. Dinner is ready and gettin' cold," I tell them.

They walk up to me all skins and jeans. Covered in grease and dirt. They've been working on their cars as usual. "What's for dinner?" Wolf asks me. Getting a little closer than I would prefer.

"Ribs," I reply.

"Yes!" they both shout. I shake my head and we all walk inside. We all sit down and eat. When we finish a rib we give the bone to Roxy. She knaws on the bones and begs for another when she finishes one. I shoo her away and she walks around the table until one of us give her a bone.

After dinner I shower. Snake walks in and starts brushing his teeth. "Thanks for the burst of cold air," I holler over the running water.

"There is one bathroom besides Mommas," he says. "It's this one and I am not usin' Mommas bathroom."

"She doesn't have cooties, she's your mother Snake," I hiss at him. "You bathed in her bathroom before. It's just brushing your teeth."

"Hell no, I am not goin' in there," he sneers at me. "Oh and hurry up, hot water only lasts so long in here."

I huff heavily at him and he walks out and I continue my shower. Afterward I sit on my bed. All

I think about is Isaiah. Nobody can know about us. I've snuck around with guys before but not for a real relationship. This is all new to me. And new to Isaiah. I mean yeah we've had relationships before but only sexual relationships. And those are one night stands ninety percent of the time. Us as an actual relationship couple is all new. I don't know what I'm feeling but Isaiah does.

Stop that non-sense! You love him and he loves you. Don't deny yourself this Sheryl. Because I'm winning and you know it!

I sigh heavily and flop down on my bed in my usual night clothes. Yes, internal battle, you are winning. I hate that she's winning.

But Isaiah is Isaiah. He's a straight forward guy. He tells you what he feels and it's always the truth. All I know is he loves me. Me of all people. I never thought I was lovable but to Isaiah I am. I am his and he is mine. I've longed for this for so long. The way he held me today, I loved it. The kiss we shared before we parted ways for the evening, it took my breath away.

As I lay in bed starring at the off white ceiling, all I can think about is when am I going to see him again. Hopefully soon like I told him.

I look at my phone. It's after midnight. I put it on the charger and curl up on my side. I close my eyes and start to drift. The thought plays on my mind. As sleep pulls me under I barely whisper, "I love Isaiah."

Chapter 4

I wake just a little after three AM. I look at my phone. Of course Isaiah texts me. "If you're reading this don't bother going back to sleep. Come to Cliff Point."

Of course he always wants to meet up at odd times but I can't sleep. I never have been able to sleep. I wake up at odd times every night and then never go back to sleep. I usually end up going to Cliff Point. And Isaiah knows this because he's been watching me for six months.

I pull on some jeans and then my denim jacket with no top. I sleep in my bra and thong. I'd rather bare most of me than none. I grab my phone and car keys. Careful not to wake Snake as I walk past his room, I sneak out. They all know I can't sleep but Snake will question it if he hears me sneaking out. He is very nosey when it comes to my where abouts. I wish he wasn't because I end up saying something or pissing both of us off.

I make it passed Snakes room and over to the front door. Careful not to make it creak, I slip through the door and over to my car. I crank it and make my way to Cliff Point. Why on earth he wants to meet I don't know. But I want to see him. I feel my adrenaline spike as I get closer to Cliff Point. Sneaking around with someone gives me a thrill. One I've never had before. And I love this new thrill.

If finally admitting you love him gives you a thrill, then by golly I do believe I have won yet again,

Sheryl. I just grin and shake my head and give in to my internal battle. For the first time.

As I pull into Cliff Point I see him. Just him. His car is two shades darker than mine so it's hard to see it at night. I turn my car off then get out. He sees what I'm wearing and I notice his eyes turn from bright gray to molten gray in a split second. He grabs me. I smirk seductively at him.

"You wore this on purpose," he growls. His lips curl into a carnal smile and he runs his hand across my back side.

"No, I just threw some clothes on," I tell him. "I sleep practically nude. Except for my bra and thong. I pulled on some jeans and my jacket and got here as quick as I could."

His hands move to my rear and he squeezes. He moans then his lips are on mine. I place my hands on his chest and tug at his shirt. He comes even closer to me and I moan when I feel him just above my hip. One of his hands moves to the nape of my neck and he grabs my hair and pulls my head back. "Do you know what you do to me?" he growls.

"Oh yes I do, and I'm glad I do it, too," I smirk at him. He grins and presses his lips to mine. "You wanna do something or just make out?" I ask him as he kisses my neck to my collar bone.

"Oh baby, I thought you would never ask," he says and lifts me up. "Kick your shoes off," he orders me. I do as he says and kick them off. "Now wrap your legs around me." I wrap my legs around his waist and he sets my bottom on the hood of his car. He goes back to kissing my neck and I moan. He pushes my jacket off my shoulders and a breeze hits me and I shiver. He smiles then his lips find mine. I slip my hands under his shirt. Just feeling his toned muscles drives me crazy.

My internal battle has silenced herself for the first time in six months. Right now, I'm glad she has. She would kill the mood and make me angry like she always does.

Isaiah moans and tugs at my lip. I smile and kiss him passionately.

It's a Monday night. Nobody but me comes to Cliff Point on a Monday night. So me and Isaiah are completely alone. Isaiah stops and looks at me. His eyes ablaze, fire gray eyes pierce into my blue-green ones. "We have two options," he starts. "One we can keep going right here and have sex on the hood. Or we can move this in the car and do more inappropriate things." I bite my lip. "Car it is then," he smirks and lifts me up.

He opens the car door and sets me down. I crawl to the back seat and lay down the way I normally do when he gets me in his car. He lays on top of me and kisses me. In the next few moments I'm clinging to him. My nails scratch at his back as I call out his name. His body goes ridged and he calls out my name. He kisses me gently then sits next to me.

"Sit up," he tells me. I do as he says and he puts an arm under my knees and one behind my back and sets me on his lap. I wrap my arms around his neck. I close my eyes and breathe him in. Gah he smells amazing. "Claw, we can do this. Sneak around. Nobody will know. We can make Monday nights our night," he whispers.

"Okay, sounds like a plan," I reply. "Monday night would work because nobody comes here on Monday nights."

"Exactly," he says. It stays silent for a while. A long while. Only the sound of us breathing is the only noise around us. "I had to see you," Isaiah says to break the silence.

"I wanted to see you," I tell him. *Tell him you love him!* And she's back, I scowl at her and she scowls back. She will never let up until I say it.

"I knew you came here when you couldn't sleep, so I figured I would see if you would meet me here," he explains.

I pull a cigarette out and light it. "Like I said, I wanted to see you. Since you told me you watched me out here I knew you would be here. I woke up not long after you texted me," I explain. He nods and takes the cigarette from me. "Isaiah how do you really feel about me?" I ask him.

Oh my God Sheryl! You know how he feels about you! I shove her away and listen to what Isaiah says.

"I love you," he says. His grip on me tightens. I nuzzle his neck and I feel him smile. "How do you feel about me?" he asks. His tone serious.

"I love you Isaiah," I tell him. *Thank you! Finally you admit it!* I can't help but smile at my internal battle. She has won again, yes but this time I wanted her to.

He kisses me lightly. I start making it a passionate kiss. His hands go to my waist. I put my legs on either side of him. He moans and I moan back. My phone vibrates but I ignore it. I'm with Isaiah and nothing else matters.

My phone stops then starts again. "Damn what do people want with you?" Isaiah asks me. Anger evident in his voice.

"I don't know," I hiss at him. I pull my phone out. "Shit its Snake," I swear. Isaiah gets quiet. "What Snake?" I snap when I answer the phone.

"Are you at Cliff Point?" he asks me.

"Yeah, where else do I go when I can't sleep?"

"Just curious. I saw you sneak past my room a few hours ago. Wolf heard ya car so I called to check up on ya," he explains.

Shit! He saw me. And Wolf heard my car. "Well mind your own damn business," I snap. "I'll come back in a little while. Before momma wakes up."

"Okay, just be safe," he tells me.

"Yeah, yeah whatever," I say and hang up the phone. "Shit, I gotta go," I tell Isaiah.

He pulls me to him and kisses me. "I had fun tonight," he whispers. I smile. "And from the looks of that smile you did too," he laughs. "Just wish you didn't have to go so soon. We have all night."

"I did have fun," I reply with a smile and kiss him. "I wish I could stay all night, too. But if I'm not back soon, like I said, Snake'll come lookin' for you and me and catch us. And we can't afford that."

"I wish you didn't have to go but we can't risk getting caught," he says. "I can't risk losing you either." I pull my jeans on and step out of his car. Isaiah follows me and pulls me to him again. "When do you want to meet up again?" he asks me. A small, hopeful gleam in his eyes. He looks every bit the eighteen year old boy I'm in love with.

"Whenever you want to, I mean every other day of the week this place is full of people," I explain. "I hope it's soon though," I add with a smirk.

He grins back. "We'll figure something out. In the meantime, stay clothed," he says. "I always protect what's mine you know that. And you are mine so keep your clothes on."

"You can't stop me when I go to bed," I smirk at him.

"No, but in public I can," he growls.

"Jeez message received," I say. He nods.

"I'll see ya soon," he whispers and kisses me.

"I'll see ya soon," I repeat. He releases me and I put my jacket and shoes back on then get in my car. He waves as I drive away.

Damn Snake for ruining our night. I look at my phone, it's five AM. Momma Jeanine wakes up around eight. Plenty of time for me to get home and be in bed asleep before she wakes up. Wait what am I thinking? This is Momma Jeanine she doesn't care if I'm in bed. Or asleep. She's not Carla. I ease off the gas and notice Isaiah's car tops the hill. I turn down the dirt road to Snake's place and notice his car stops at the end. When he is no longer in my vision I feel upset. I wonder if Isaiah feels the same.

You know he does! But then again, he might not. Sheryl this is a hard decision. You need to ask him when you can. And now my internal battle has changed her mind. I shake my head at her and frown. I don't want to think of Isaiah not feeling the same about me.

I park my car and walk inside. Snake meets me at his bedroom door. "Sex hair," he says matter of factly.

I run my fingers through my hair to tame it. "For all you know I rode in my car with the windows down," I sneer.

"I know sex hair and that, Claw, is sex hair," he tells me. "Who with and why?" he questions. Always so inquisitive.

49

He can't find out about me and Isaiah though. So I tell him the partial truth. "I was alone at the cliff until Isaiah showed. I needed a good time and he gave me one," is all I say. Not entirely a lie, but enough to get Snake o stop asking about it.

"Alright, seems fishy but alright," he tells me. I nod and he walks back in his room. "Claw, I'm always watching and finding out things. If there is anything you need to tell me do it now."

"Snake if there was I would tell you," I tell him. He shuts his door without another word. Damn him and always wanting information.

I make my way to my room and close the door. I toss my jacket across the room and plop down on my bed. I wish Isaiah was here. If he was what would we be doing? Making out or having sex? I would be fine with either. Just sleeping next to him would be a treasure at this point.

I close my eyes for a few minutes. When they open again I smell breakfast. I get up and put on clothes of some form. Tight short, shorts and a tank top. I walk into the kitchen as I put my hair up in a ponytail. Momma Jeanine sits with Snake and Wolf at the table. "We waited up for ya. Figured you would want to eat with the rest of us," Momma Jeanine tells me.

"Thanks," I say and sit down.

"Damn Claw them shorts look good on you," Wolf smirks. "Especially here," he says and runs his finger across my thigh where the shorts stop.

"Back off Wolf," I hiss at him.

"Oh, so touchy all of a sudden," he says.

"Neither of us has been like that towards each other since we slept together," I snarl at him. "And we are not going to start again."

"Damn what's gotten into you?" Snake asks. I smirk to myself and think *Isaiah has gotten into me.*

Oh yes he has! My internal battle hollers and jumps for joy. *And in more ways than one! I'm winning again!*

"Nothing Snake, just don't like Wolf touchin' on me. You should know that," I reply. "Guess your trip to Cliff Point didn't really help then."

"Oh it did, just not towards Wolf," I laugh.

"Does anything work on him?" Snake laughs as he eats.

"Hell no," Momma Jeanine adds. "Even condoms couldn't prevent that boy from happening. Six million sperm and that's the one that got through." We all die laughing at the table. All of us except Wolf that is. He stares at us with his mouth agape. "It's true son, now close ya mouth and finish ya breakfast," she tells him.

"This ain't fair," he huffs. "What about Snake, huh? Got anything for him? I bet you don't 'cause he's the good one."

"Oh come on Wolf we're all havin' a little fun. Calm down and eat ya breakfast," Momma Jeanine tells him.

"Yeah bro, even though I am the good one," Snake boasts about himself. "Momma actually wanted me."

"Damn you Snake!" he hollers and throws something at his brother. "Shut ya trap or I'll shut it for ya!"

"Boys, boys!" Momma Jeannine shouts. "Both of ya stop ya squallin' and finish ya breakfast before I shut the both of ya up." They both sigh and continue eating they're breakfast.

As we eat I notice Snake staring at me. It's unnerving. Every so often he looks away but comes back to me. I'd give anything to know what he's thinking. Well except a free pass for him to sleep with me. He eats slowly. Slower than usual. Which I'm not saying he eats slow. Snake eats like a pig. All sloppy and spilling food everywhere. He cleans it all up but man its unnerving how slow he's eating this morning. And staring at me.

He might know something Sheryl. Watch yourself around him. You know that just as well as anyone does! I know, I know internal battle. Keep quiet until I have a real battle to discuss internally. Jeez she's getting on my nerves lately.

I get up from the table and make my way to my room. I light up a cigarette once I'm in my room and open up the window. I sit with one leg in the house and the other out. Snake walks in my room and closes the door. "What the hell do you want Snake?" I ask him as I exhale smoke.

"To talk," he says and closes the door.

"About?" I ask him. "If it's about me going to Cliff Point I told you all that happened," I tell him.

"It is about Cliff Point but not about what you did there," he says. "You only snap on Wolf like that unless you two are sleeping together," he explains.

"Shit Snake we are not sleeping together. I've only slept with Isaiah in the past week," I explain. "The past year actually," I say more to myself.

"Just thought I would ask," he says. "You and Isaiah huh? What's going on with you two?" he asks.

"Nothing is going on between us," I tell him. "We're just hooking up every now and then. He has a lot to offer a girl. So he's my go to guy for sex," I lie coolly. Isaiah would be proud of that lie.

"Okay, just steer clear of him otherwise," he warns me. "If I find out there is something more I'll beat his ass," Snake says as he walks out of my room.

"Yeah, yeah," is all I say. I put my cigarette out and close the window. I slipped it passed him for now but he'll find out eventually. And when he does it will not be pretty. There is no telling what he will do if he finds out but it will be bad.

I need to see Isaiah though. I know it's only been a few hours since I saw him but I can't stand to be away from him. I text him asking him when we can meet again. There is no reply but he's probably busy. He drives all the time. It's what he does to relieve his stress. I set my phone aside and go sit in the window again. I stare into the back yard and watch Roxy roll around in the grass. I remember being a kid running around in the grass with my dad. Before he left me alone with Carla.

Being a child was carefree. No worries, I loved it. Then I became a teen and realized that the world is shitty and Frank was an abusive ass. I knew he would leave eventually.

Carla hasn't bothered to call me since she told me my last check came in the mail. Which I'm glad. Maybe she finally realizes that she doesn't need me all the time. Or in her life.

"Claw! Someone is here for you!" Snake yells across the house.

"Yeah, yeah," I say. "I'm coming." I walk out of my room and into the living room. "Who wants to talk to me and why?" I snap.

"Carla is at the door. She wants to talk you," Snake tells me as he points to the door. She's not allowed to walk in Snakes house so she stands on the porch all the time.

"Why does she want to talk to me?" I ask them. They all shrug and I huff. I walk over to the door and open it. "What do you want?" I spit at her.

"To talk," she tells me.

"About?" I ask her.

"I want you to come back home," she tells me. I go to speak but she stops me. "Hear me out Sheryl, please."

"Okay fine," I tell her.

I walk outside and we sit on the porch swing. It gets quiet for a few minutes. What is she gonna say and why?

The cool breeze blows through, blowing my hair away from my neck. The silence is stifling. I hate silence with Carla. Nothing good comes of silence with her.

"The house is empty without you in it," she explains. "Please come home. I know you're almost nineteen and you are a legal adult but please come home."

"No," I say simply. "I've lived with you long enough Carla. I live here now. Go back home and don't ever come looking for me again," I tell her. I turn to walk inside and she grabs me. Her hand gripping my arm tightly. Now she's using force? Seems like a very Frank thing to do to get what she wants. "Let go!" I snap at her. She lets me go and we just stare at each other.

"I'll buy you a car," she says quickly.

"You see that over there," I point to my car. "I have one. And no amount of bribery will get me to come back home," I add. And with that I slam the door in her face.

Chapter 5

"What did Carla want?" Snake asks me. He's sitting on the couch with Momma Jeannine and Wolf. All of them wanting to know what Carla said to me.

"Me to come back home," I say simply. "She said she would buy me a car if I came back home. I don't like being bribed to do anything. She knows that." Besides she couldn't buy me if she tried. She uses bribes to get her way all the time. The only time she doesn't is when it comes to work and me.

"Well lunch'll be ready in an hour. I'll fix whatever ya want," Momma Jeanine says with a smile on her face.

In case I haven't already, Momma Jeannine is an older woman. She's older than Carla by six years. She had Snake and Wolf late in life. Her hair, turning gray from old age along with the stress her two boys put her under. She has wrinkles around her eyes and mouth. Laugh lines she calls them. Momma Jeannine has always been a happy woman. According to her there has never been a dull moment in her life. Or a moment that made her frown or cry. Before her husband past, she was a bright cheerful woman. Her brown eyes alight with pure joy.

Snake remembers those days. Wolf not so much. Wolf always ran around and was rarely home. But when her husband past, as Snake would say: "it's like the end of the world for her. Pa, was the only man who made her happy. The world ended and fell away at her feet the day he died." After that, only me and the boys keep her going.

"Thanks," I tell her. "Rib sandwich would be nice."

"Sounds like a plan Claw," she says. "Boys what do you want?" she asks Snake and Wolf.

"Same," both reply. Momma Jeanine nods and gets up and heads to the kitchen. As long as she busies herself, she stays happy. It's when she's just sitting and thinking does she go into a quiet, depressed state.

I walk back to my room and sit in the window again. With my phone in hand, I just stare at it. Damn Carla and always wanting me in her life. Why can't she just forget me like she forgot my father? She has never done me any good nor will she do me any good. I am finally free. Free and away from her.

Free as a bird? Maybe not, Sheryl. You have Isaiah to think about and whether he feels the same when he leaves you and doesn't know when he'll see you again. Not being free. Why can't I just have a normal conscience? Mine is always up my ass battling me about everything. I sigh and look away from my phone.

I take a glance at the mirror by the window. My dyed black hair is fading. My natural color breaking through. I need to buy hair dye and dye it again. My phone goes off with a text from Isaiah. "Whenever you want," he replies.

Because that so helps the situation. I sigh and reply with a simple okay. He calls me. "Claw, we have to keep this a secret. If we meet up too much people will suspect and Snake will find out."

"Yeah, I know that," I tell him. Careful not to say his name out loud, Snake could be listening. "Well there's gonna be a big group of us at Cliff Point tonight. I guess I'll see you there."

"You will, I might be a little late but I'll be there," he says. I smile a little. "I'll see ya later babe."

"Alright, see you later," I say then hang up. *Babe! He called you babe! I guess I'll back off for now.* I smile as big as I can. Something finally shut her up.

I hop down from the window and walk into the living room. "Is lunch ready?" I ask.

"It is now," Momma Jeanine smiles at me as I walk into the kitchen. We all nod and go sit at the table to eat.

"There's a big group of us goin' to Cliff Point tonight," Snake says. "Word around is there's a bunch of new kids comin'."

"Oh really? Think I need to show them a thing or two," I reply with an edge to my voice. New kids always need showing the ways of Cliff Point. My internal battle shakes her head at me. She hates when I fight people. It's who I am. She can get over it.

"Claw, these new kids, supposedly, ain't afraid of nothin'," Wolf tells me as he shovels food in his mouth. "Apparently they are total bad asses. People not to be messed with."

"We'll see after tonight," I reply slyly. "Besides they haven't met me have they?" I say and graze my nails down Wolf's face. Just light enough I don't scratch him.

"Claw get those things away from me," he warns. His eyes wide with panic.

"What is Wolf afraid imma scratch his precious baby face?" I ask and flick my nails away from his face. He grabs at his face like I hurt him. We all bust out laughing.

"Man Wolf, are you that afraid of her?" Snake asks him.

"You would be too if she's slapped you before with those nails!" he exclaims.

"Oh yeah, I remember that," Momma Jeanine says. "You showed him that day," she laughs.

That was three months after I slept with Wolf. He wanted another go around and I said no. He grabbed me and started jerking me around so I slapped him and left claw marks on his face. They were there for two months. Pretty deep, too if I remember correctly.

"They're still there!" he hollers and points at his face. "Do you know how hard that is telling people I got my ass handed to me by a girl?"

"What time we leavin'?" I ask. Blatantly ignoring Wolf and his outburst about the scars I left on him.

"Dusk," Snake says as he shovels food in his mouth. "Oh, and I heard Isaiah is comin'. Odd for him to show twice in two weeks." I just nod and finish my lunch.

Dusk comes all too soon. Me, Snake, and Wolf drive our own cars to Cliff Point. I get there first. There's already tons of people here. I start to see a few I don't recognize. Snake and Wolf pull in behind me. They walk over to me and we lean on my car. I don't see Isaiah's car. I know he said he would be late but I hope not too late. "There," Wolf points to a group walking towards us. "Is the new guys." All of them dressed in letterman's jackets and light colored blue jeans. Every bit the college kid look. I hate them already

"They look like college kids," Snake snarls. I see him throw his cigarette butt to the ground violently.

"What the fuck are stingy college kids doin' at Cliff Point?" I growl. I hate college kids; they're just a step above high school ass holes.

"They're not, from what I've been told," Wolf says. "Wanna be college kids. That is what they are," he explains. Me and Snake nod.

The new guys approach us and stand about two feet away. "We heard you three basically run the place," a blonde haired guy says.

"Yeah," I say and inhale off my cigarette. "We do." Real casual talk is not my thing but imma let it slide. For now.

"My name's Josh, that's Fox, Charlie, and Razor," the blonde says.

"Oh so you come with nicknames already?" I question in a sarcastic tone. Snake and Wolf laugh. They know what I'm about to do. I step away from my car and begin to circle them. I became the "leader", if you will, of Cliff Point shortly after I came here. Every one respects me here.

"You see boys, how things work around Cliff Point is you get nicknames when you get here. You do not come with a nickname got that?"

"Oh yeah? What are you gonna do about it whore?" Blondie asks me. Him and his friends chuckle.

Anger rises inside me. I grab blondie's shirt collar and get in his face. "First off the name's Claw," I growl. "And second you are on MY turf. You respect me and all my friends here or ya leave. I am the leader here. What I say goes, got that Blondie?"

"Who left you in charge huh?" he asks me. "If you ask me you look like a girl who needs her Mommy more than she needs to be here," he sneers. It's getting darker by the minute. I don't wanna fight these guys but looks like I might have to if Blondie doesn't shut his fucking mouth. "Oh Mommy save me all these guys want to have sex with me," he says like a scared little girl.

"They all smoke Mommy, smoking is bad, save me," Carrot Top, aka Charlie, says.

"You guys might wanna watch yourself," Snake warns.

"Why? She couldn't harm a fly," Fox grins in my direction. I know that grin. The I-wanna-sleep-with-her grin. All guys use it. It doesn't bother me though.

"You're a pretty little thing, why don't I show you a good time," Razor says and reaches around to grab my ass.

I hear Isaiah's car. I've gotta do something about this guy touching me. Not just for Isaiah's sake but the fact that no one touches me.

Razor grabs my hand and I snatch it from him. I'm getting angrier by the second. I can feel the heat from my anger radiating off of me. He grabs at me again and I lunge at him. "You don't ever fucking touch me!" I yell and punch him. I scratch at his face and then the other three guys are on me.

I pull away from them and scratch each one of them. Blondie goes to hit me but I duck and kick him hard. I slam him to the ground and punch him over and over. My anger becoming more prominent. Carrot Top pulls me away but I bite his hand and throw him over my shoulder. I scratch him from his face down his chest. Ripping and shredding hi shirt as I go.

Fox grabs at me and goes to hit me. He hits my nose. Blood gushes from it but I don't let it stop me. My adrenaline is high. Nothing can stop me. I scratch him on both sides of his face. He screams out in pain.

By this point everyone has gathered around in a huge circle to watch me beat these guys asses. Everyone cheering me on. It's one against four. Well more like three. Blondie is down for the count. He fell first. Not much of a fight in him. Carrot Top comes at me again but I hit him with an upper cut and down he goes. Just me against Fox and Razor. Both circling me.

"Come on, hit me!" I yell, blood and spit flying from my mouth. "Do it! Fucking hit me!" Both of them stop where they are and drop to their knees. I wipe the blood from my nose. Snake hands me a towel from my car. "From now on you four will address me as Claw got that? Y'all have the claw marks to prove it!"

"Yes ma'am," they all say weakly.

"Now get the fuck up," I spit. "Everyone take a good look at them!" I holler. "This is what will happen if any one of you, or any new person, touches me. I will leave scars of my claw marks on your faces." Everyone nods and the circle dissipates. "Your four, here. Now," I order them. They limp over to me and attempt to look at me. "Your new name is Carrot Top, yours is Blondie, and you two may keep the name you came with," I tell them. They all nod. "Now scram!"

All of them attempt to run from me. I laugh as they do. All limps and bleeding.

"Good job Claw, showing them who's boss," Snake cheers and gives me a high five. I wince with pain as he slaps my hand. "You okay?" he asks me.

"I think I broke my hand punching them," I say. I flex my hand and it hurts. Pain radiates from it. "Get me something to wrap it with," I tell Snake. He nods and rips a towel into a strip to wrap around my hand. He wraps it carefully around my hand then ties it off. "Thanks, I'll get Momma to look at it when we get home," I say. They both nod.

I look over to see Isaiah smirking at me. "I'm gonna go see Isaiah," I say and walk off.

I get to his car and he grabs my injured hand. "Broken hand huh? I'm glad you showed them whose boss," he says. "And a broken nose? Damn you put up a fight tonight didn't you?" he asks with laughter in his voice.

Great, he's laughing at you. I shoot my internal battle an evil look and she cowers in fear back to a dark corner of my brain.

"Well when people touch what's not there's shit gets real and punches get thrown," I explain. "And claw marks become scars," I add and curl my tongue around my words and grin at him.

"You wanna do something?" he asks me. "Like get in my car and howl to the moon in utter pleasure?"

he smirks at me. His eyes start turning a molten gray color. The constant intensity change in the color is so amazing. It drives me crazy.

"Oh I always do, you know that," I smirk back. He grabs my ass and squeezes. I moan.

"Do what you always do, nobody will suspect if you do what you always do," he whispers in my ear. I nod and slip my shoes and jacket off. He puts them in his trunk and I climb inside his car. "Sit up," he tells me. I look at him with a quizzical look. "We are doing things a little different tonight," he tells me.

"Uhh...okay?" I say a little confused. Different how? *Sheryl he loves you, just follow him and do as he says. For all you know he's about to drop a marriage bomb.*

"Remember where we left off Monday night?" he asks me. I nod. "That's where we are starting off tonight," he grins.

Marriage bomb? That was stupid on my part. Hehe, I'll say that was close! Shut it internal battle. I'm having my time with my man. And at that, my internal battle has zipped her lips and sat down.

I sit on his lap with my legs on either side of him. He starts kissing me then works his way down my neck to my collar bone. "Oh Isaiah," I moan. In no time we are both breathing heavily and I'm howling. I'm sure everyone can hear me but I don't care. Isaiah holds me to him in the after math. I burry my head in his neck and try to catch my breath.

"If only we could have finished that Monday." I can hear the smirk in his voice.

I sit up and look at him. "Probably wouldn't have been as good," I smirk and kiss him. "Anticipation for another makes it stronger."

"That it does," he smirks at me. "Let me see your hand," he says. I give him my hand and he unwraps it. He pushes on various places and I wince and flinch when he does. He looks at me and giggles. "Does it hurt that bad?"

"Yes, it does," I tell him.

"Don't be a pansy," he grins at me.

"I am not a pansy!" I whisper shout at him and slap his chest.

He kisses the palm of my hand then wraps it again. Then his face gets serious. "Ice it when you get back to Snake's place. I'd wrap it in something better than a towel though."

"I intend to," I tell him. He hands me my clothes and I put them on. "I'll text you later," I tell him.

"Okay, be careful with that hand," he warns me. Before I get out of his car, he holds me to him. "You're so beautiful," he whispers. He kisses me gently.

"You're not bad lookin' yourself," I reply and leave a swift, chaste kiss on his lips. He smacks my ass and I yelp.

"Ha! Every time!" he exclaims. I slap his chest playfully and wince. He looks sternly at me, "please be careful." Enunciating every word so I know he means it.

I get out of his car and he follows me. "I will don't worry," I tell him. He hands me my shoes and my jacket. "Thanks," I say.

"No problem," he grins. He pulls me to him once more and squeezes my ass. "This is mine," he warns. "Nobody else touches what's mine. And stay clothed."

"Why do you think I beat the shit out of those guys Isaiah? They touched me," I explain. "And I know to stay clothed," I retort. For a few seconds we just stand there starring at each other. Gah he's so perfect. And all mine.

"Good girl," he smirks and winks at me. He releases me. "Talk to you soon," he whispers. I nod and walk off.

"Have a good time?" Snake smirks at me. "'Cause from all the howlin' we heard, sounds like ya did."

"Always do with Isaiah," I smile.

"Come on then, it's nearing five in the morning. Let's go home," Wolf says. Me and Snake nod and get in our cars. I wave by to Isaiah and drive off.

We reach home and I walk inside and Momma Jeanine notices my hand and my nose. She instantly gets to work on fixing me up. "Snake get me the first aid kit will ya," she orders him. He nods and walks off. He comes back and sets it on the table. She takes the towel off my hand and looks at it then touches it lightly.

"Damn!" I yell and snatch my hand from her. My adrenalin as completely worn off and I feel all pain. In my hand and my nose.

"Claw give me ya hand so I can wrap it," she says sternly. I give her my hand and she rubs something on it then wraps it. "It's not broken just sprained," she tells me. "Let me see ya nose," she says. She touches it in several places along the bridge and I flinch. "This is broken however," she tells me and puts something across my nose.

"Thanks Momma," I say quietly.

"No problem Claw, what did ya do anyway?" she asks. "Put up a good fight from what I can tell," she adds with a slight grin.

"New guys had a problem with the way I run things," I tell her. "They sure as hell don't now." I start laughing at my own statement.

"Claw showed'em, beat their asses and gave 'em new nicknames," Snake adds. "You have very rightfully earned up to a nickname. I'm glad this one stuck."

Believe me, I am too. My internal battle sighs and glares at me like I'm the one that made up the past four I had.

"She went total bad ass if ya ask me," Wolf says as he pops open a beer.

"I always do when people touch me like that guy did," I snarl.

"Hey, calm down now," Momma Jeanine tells us. "Off to bed with the three of ya. Normally I would say you'd be fine but Claw ya need the sleep. You three have been out all night, bed," she orders us.

"Yes ma'am," we all say. Wolf puts up the first aid kit and we walk to our rooms.

I'm beyond tired. I'm exhausted. I could have fallen asleep in Isaiah's arms in his car. But then people would find out about us.

Then Snake would kill him! He's starting to find out things! I shun her, bitch needs to keep her mouth shut.

I strip and lay in bed in just my under clothes like I always do. I reach over and plug my phone into the charger and curl up under the sheets. I breathe in and exhale heavily. I did steal Isaiah's pull over before I left. Snake didn't recognize it. It makes sleep come easily, feeling close to Isaiah. Breathing in his scent on his pull over. All sweat and the hint of fresh laundry. It sells of Isaiah. Of comfort.

It feels good to finally go to sleep. Even though it won't be for long. Maybe if Isaiah slept next to me I could sleep for a longer amount of time. I don't know. The thought makes me smile a little. I sigh again and sleep takes over.

Chapter 6

I wake a few hours later. Or at least what seems a few hours. I look at my phone. It's almost three in the afternoon. I gasp and jump up. I realize I have nothing to really do today so I sink back into bed. I can't go see Isaiah, I wish I could. I miss him terribly. I close my eyes and start to drift again when my door opens. "Claw get up," Wolf tells me.

"Why should I?" I ask sleepily. "I got nothin' better to do."

"Because, Momma bought you more hair dye and she wants to dye your hair today," he explains. "Now get up." He kicks at my bed and it shakes violently.

"Fuck off Wolf," I holler and throw a pillow at him. I flip him off and he flips m off back.

"Then get up or I'll carry you," he orders. I huff and get up. "Nice bra," he smirks and closes the door before I can throw something else at him.

Isaiah would not approve! "Oh shut it, internal bitch," I hiss at her. I know he wants me clothed. Maybe even at night while I'm here I should wear more clothes to bed. *I think Isaiah would sleep better knowing you were clothed all the time!* I growl at her and she stands her ground and glares back at me. I huff and pull myself out of bed.

I put some clothes on and walk into the kitchen. "Momma you didn't have to buy that for me I would have bought it," I tell her as I sit down.

"I saw ya hair goin' back to its original color so I figure I'd buy it and dye it for ya," she tells me. "Blackest black right?" she asks me.

"Yep," I reply. She nods and starts dying my hair.

"Snake put gas in ya car this morning," she tells me. "There is a whole carton of Marlboro Reds for ya on the counter. And I bought two more boxes of this hair dye just in case."

"You guys don't have to do all this for me. I have the money to do it," I tell her. "All Frank's child support checks pay off."

"It's what family does for each other. And Claw you're family," she explains. "Always have been. And always will be."

I smile at this. I've always been family to them I've just never heard them actually tell me I'm family. I feel wanted here. Like someone should feel around family. Unlike I did at Carla's. even if I am biologically her child.

Snake and Wolf walk in covered in car grease and smell of oil. They walk passed me and Momma and sit on the couch. Something is wrong. Way wrong and I can sense it. *They know about you and Isaiah! Someone is feeding them information!*

They begin to talk to each other in hushed voices. Every so often Snake glances at me then looks back at Wolf. Momma tilts my head down and I can no longer see them. But I can still hear them. I'm not sure what they're talking about but it seems serious. I can feel Snakes cold glare pierce through me.

"To the bathroom we go," she tells me.

I've sat for twenty-five minutes with hair dye in my hair listening to Snake and Wolf whisper to each other. I've gathered bits and pieces of information on what they are talking about. It has to deal with me and some guy. Shit! I hope they didn't find out about me and Isaiah.

They have! The two of them know! I start getting worried. They can't know about me and him. Whoever's talking needs to shut their mouth.

"Momma do you know what Snake and Wolf are talking about?" I ask her as she rinses my hair. Just on the off chance that she might know something that I don't know.

"Not a clue 'cept it's about you," she tells me. "You and some boy named Isaiah."

I start to panic. They've found out. How? Me and Isaiah were keeping quiet. Or at least I thought we were. Momma Jeanine finishes with my hair and I towel dry it. She tells me to sit outside to let it dry.

I do as she says and sit on the porch. I text Isaiah. "Snake and Wolf know something about us. I'm not sure what yet."

He replies quickly. "How could they find out? We've kept our cool."

"I don't know Isaiah, I don't know." My phone stays silent. I hear snake and Wolf make their way to the porch. I quickly delete mine and Isaiah's messages. They'll never know if they look through my phone. No evidence, no proof.

"Claw we need to talk," Snake says. Damn, cuttin' straight to the point.

"What about huh?" I snarl at him.

"You and Isaiah," he growls. "You two are doing more than just sleeping together. Sneaking around. Always seeing each other. And he showed at Cliff Point last night unexpectedly. He hardly ever comes to Cliff Point."

"What are you two getting at?" I ask them. "I only see Isaiah when I need sex," I explain. I light up a cigarette and stick it between my lips.

"Claw you know how we deal with him if he hurts you," Wolf says. "That fucker won't see the light of day again if he does."

"Nothing is going on between us," I snap at them. "If there was it would be weird. Nobody from Cliff Point dates. Except Logan and Roxy."

"They were datin' before they go to the Cliff," Wolf adds.

"Claw tell us, we know things," Snake says. "Something is going on between you two. People are dropping little bits of info. Just tell us!"

"Oh my God Snake nothing is going on between me and Isaiah," I tell him. "What makes you think something is going on between me and him?"

"Somebody saw you two makin' out," Wolf says. "In the middle of the day at Cliff Point. Then some other people saw you together Monday night. Word is getting out Claw. Speak up now or we will find him," Wolf threatens.

"Why hurt him? It's not gonna do any good," I tell them. *You're slipping! Don't give away too much!*

"Oh so now you're defending him? So you are together?" Snake interrogates.

"We are not together Snake," I say. I know what Snake and Wolf will do if they find out about me and Isaiah. If they don't kill him they'll injure him for sure.

"Claw last chance," Wolf says.

"What's it gonna be? Speak up or forever hold ya piece," Snake hisses.

"Oh so know this is a wedding ceremony?" I say sarcastically.

"Shut up Claw just answer us," he spits.

"Nothing is going on between us!" I holler.

"Fine," Wolf growls.

"Next piece of information we get we're going after him. And if he is your precious boyfriend we'll fuck him up," Snake threatens.

With that they walk inside and leave me alone. I light up another cigarette and smoke it. I take the towel around my neck inside. I grab my keys and get in my car. I drive somewhere. I don't know where. Anywhere but here.

I drive slow passed Cliff Point and notice Isaiah's car is there. He sees my car and waves. I drive over to him. "We need to talk," I tell him. "Get in."

He doesn't hesitate. He gets in my car and I speed off. "You mind telling me what we need to talk about?" he asks me. "Slow down Claw, damn."

I take my foot off the gas and slow down some. "Snake and Wolf know," I tell him. Glancing in all directions to make sure we're not being followed by anyone. My paranoia reaching a new level every second that passes.

"Know what? How could they know?" he asks me. "We've been keeping quiet. Layin' low so no one catches us."

"People are feeding them information," I tell him. "People saw us they day we got together. They saw us Monday night," I tell him. "People are finding out and coming to Snake and Wolf about it. Then Snake and Wolf are looking at me about the whole thing." I turn down a dirt road that dead ends.

"Claw what are you doing?" he asks me. "Where are we going?"

I stop my car and put it in park. I put my head on the steering wheel and sigh. I feel Isaiah's hand touch my back. He runs it up and down my back softly. I start to cry. "All I've ever wanted is a family who loves me for who I am and the decisions I make. I thought moving into Snake's would bring me that. I got the family part but not the love I wanted."

"Hey, calm down," Isaiah whispers. "Come here." He pulls me into his lap and holds me. He holds me the way I've wanted to be held for a while.

"I want everything to work out right for a change and nothing has. I run into a dead end all the time," I sob. I don't usually cry. But when I do it's because I've kept it bottled inside for a while. "Nobody understands me. Ever since my dad left I've been left to fin for myself. Nobody loves me."

"That's not true," he whispers.

"Yes it is," I sob.

"No it's not and you want me to tell you why it's not true?" he asks me. I nod. "I love you," he says. "I understand you. I've been left on my own since I was twelve," he explains. "My father left when I was ten. I know what it's like," he explains.

Breakthrough! I'm winning again!

"You really love me?" I ask him. I sit back to look at him. *Ugh!* My internal battle sighs and sinks to the floor. *Why question him?*

"Yes I really love you," he says. "And you don't need Snake's family to make you feel loved. You have me. I'll be your family. From now to the ends of the Earth. Nothing will keep me from you or change the way I look at you. Not even a broken nose and a broken hand can stop me from loving you," he says. He tucks a strand of hair behind my ear. It makes me grin.

"You mean that?"

"With all of my heart," he whispers. "You are my one and only."

"Oh Isaiah," I say and kiss him. "And you are mine," I whisper.

I feel him smile as I kiss him. I pull away and lay my head in the crook of his neck. Isaiah continues to rub my back. I start to fall asleep in his arms.

"Have you slept lately?" he asks me. I shake my head no. "Let's lay down in the back and I'll lay with you while you sleep." I nod and get off his lap. We lay in the backseat of my car and Isaiah holds me to him. "Go to sleep Claw," he whispers. I nod and close my eyes.

I open my eyes to the sunlight peering in my car window. Isaiah has a tight grip on me. How long have I been asleep? I'm not sure. I feel great though. Isaiah wakes up and looks at me. "Good morning beautiful," he says sleepily.

"Good morning," I reply with a smile. "How long have we been asleep?" I ask him.

"Since five o'clock yesterday," he replies. "It's currently," he starts and looks at his phone. "Nine o'clock in the morning the next day," he tells me.

"Oh shit," I say and sit up. "I've gotta get back before Snake and Wolf go looking for me then you."

Which they probably already have. Get going!

"Can't we just lay here for a little while longer?" he asks me. He kisses me softly and I smile.

"I wish we could but I gotta go," I tell him.

"Okay," he says with a sad face. "Don't forget I gotta get my car from Cliff Point," he reminds me.

"I know," I tell him. We climb in the front seat and I start my car. The drive to Cliff Point is silent. Neither of us wants to part ways but we have to so we don't get caught. Although some people already suspect something is going on between us. I stop my car beside Isaiah's car and he kisses me softly.

"I had a good time last night," he tells me.

"Me too," I reply with a smile. "I'll text you later."

"Okay," he says. He gets out of my car and then turns to me. "Claw," he starts.

"Yeah?" I ask him.

"I love you," he smiles. A new smile. One that reaches his eyes and shows a happier, better side to him than what he always shows.

I smile back at him. "I love you, too Isaiah," I reply. He smiles even bigger then closes the door. I drive away smiling.

When I reach Snakes, Snake and Wolf come outside and stop me from going inside. "Where were you?" they ask.

"I went for a drive and slept in my car," I lie. Well partial lie.

"Sure you weren't out with Isaiah?" Snake asks me. "Remember we know things. We woulda come lookin' for ya if you hadn't showed up sooner or later."

"Probably all tangled up in skins with her lover boy, Isaiah," Wolf sneers at me.

"I think I would know if I was with someone Snake," I retort. "That's all I did was went for a drive. I slept in my car when I got tired."

"Fine," he says. "But Momma's been up all night worried about ya," he adds. "You scared her half to death."

"I'm sorry, after you two yelled at me yesterday I needed time to myself for a change. After all I am a girl. And girls need time to themselves every now and then," I reply. "I'll go apologize to Momma."

They both get out of my way and I walk inside. "Oh Sheryl I'm so glad you're okay," Momma says and hugs me. I've never seen her so worried about me before. Not even this worried for Snake or Wolf.

"I'm fine Momma, really," I tell her. "I just went for a drive. I slept in my car last night. I'm fine," I explain to her. "Just needed a little time to myself. Away from the two dip shits."

"Sometimes you have to. They do get annoying and clingy," she laughs a little. "But don't you ever do that again," she reprimands me. "Ya scared me half to death all night. Thought I lost someone else in my life."

"Yes ma'am," I say. "I'm good, though. I promise Momma." Although I will be doing that again. A couple nights here and there. Sleeping, just sleeping, in my car with Isaiah holding me close.

Soon I'll leave the house, all my things with me. Isaiah by my side driving down the road to somewhere we can be happy and together without the fear of being caught by Snake and his crazy friends.

And I won't be looking back.

Chapter 7

It's all I've been thinking about for the past few days. Running and not looking back. I haven't talked to Isaiah about it yet but I plan to tonight when I see him. Since he told me he would be my family I haven't felt the same at Snake's place. I've been going over the edge lately and yelling at them for no reason.

I've hid eight cartons of Marlboro reds so Momma Jeanine will buy me more so I don't have too. I am slowly starting to pack my things to leave. Although not enough for them to notice what I'm doing.

Snake and Wolf have kept a close eye on me lately. They have no new information about me and Isaiah so they keep tabs on me everywhere I go. They always think I'm going to Cliff Point. I'm not. I'm going to the dead end road where I took Isaiah and we slept all night in my car. I meet Isaiah somewhere and I drive to the dirt road and we either sleep all night or have sex. Though lately it's been just to sleep. Isaiah knows I don't get much.

Wish you would sleep more. It's making me too tired to fight you on your current situation. My internal battle yawns and hisses at me. She's just as tired as I am.

I walk by Snake's room and grab my car keys off the table sitting by the door. I'm meeting Isaiah at the Old Country Store. Then from there to our usual place. I have my keys in hand and make my way out the door. "Claw," Snake hisses behind me.

"What? I can't sleep I'm going to Cliff Point," I say harshly to get him off my back.

"You're not going anywhere," he says sternly. He walks over to me and grabs my arm and gets in my face. I can smell the alcohol on his breath. "You're not gonna go see'em. Momma knows what you do with him and it's my job to stop ya," he tells me. His mouth curls into an evil smile. I feel my insides shake. I quiver all over.

"Snake lemme go," I say and try to pull my arm from him. But it's impossible, he's got a strong grip on my arm.

"No, you're going back to bed and staying there," he says and starts dragging me to my room.

"Snake, dammit let me go!" I yell at him. I start to hit him and scratch at his arm. I look behind me and see Wolf and Momma Jeanine laughing menacingly at what Snake is doing. Snake turns to me and smiles an evil smile again. It's then do I notice he's walking into his room and not mine. "Snake I'm not gonna do this with you. Let me go!" I yell at him.

"Not today," he sneers and throws me on his bed. Oh please let this nightmare end. He closes the door and walks over to me.

He lays on top of me and I scream.

"Claw wake up," I hear faintly. "Babe wake up, it's okay." I'm being shaken awake. I scream and jump up. "Everything is okay. You're safe with me." I turn to see Isaiah looking at me.

"Sorry," I say and sit up. I rub my face with my hands and sigh heavily.

Oh for the love of me, don't ever dream of that again. If I can help it I won't dream of that again. That is something I never want to have happen.

"You don't have to be sorry for a nightmare," he tells me. "You wanna tell me about it?" I shake my head no. "Okay, come here," he says and pulls me to him. "What's on your mind huh? I can tell you've been thinkin' a lot lately."

"I have been," I tell him.

"Of what?" he asks me.

"Running," I say. He looks intrigued. "Leaving this place behind and going somewhere were nobody knows who I am," I explain. "I wanted to talk to you about it. See if you'd go with me."

"Who'd be the leader of Cliff Point if you left?" he asks me.

"Snake probably," I say and look down at my feet. "Or Wolf but imma go with Snake since he's the oldest."

Isaiah sighs a long heavy sigh. He runs a hand through his gorgeous black hair then looks at me. His eyes give nothing away. He's good at not showing his emotions. "Claw, if we did run what would we do for money?" he asks me.

"I've got $500,000 saved up from my father's child support money," I tell him. "I have eight cartons of Marlboro reds at Snake's place. And if you look under the seat you'll find two bottles of vodka," I tell him. "I've got the money to keep us going."

"That much huh?" he asks me. I nod. He runs a hand through his hair again. Gah what is he thinking? I would give anything to know what he's thinking. "Where would we be going?" he asks me.

"Anywhere," I tell him. "But here."

He nods. "When will we be leaving?" he asks me. The edge of his mouth turns up in a crooked smile. I've got him.

"We will be leaving as soon as possible," I tell him. "I gotta get my stuff in my car and out of Snakes place with them not home. They're gonna be gone all day in two days. I'll be the only one at his house. We'll leave then."

"Meet up at the Old Country Store, and then head out," he says. I nod. "Whose car are we taking?"

"Both, you never know when we might run into car trouble," I tell him. He nods. I look at my phone. It's only four in the morning. Enough time to fool around or sleep before I have to head back to Snakes place. I kiss Isaiah softly on his warm, soft lips. He growls low in his throat in approval.

His tongue slips in my mouth and I moan back. I sit on top of him while he's laying across the back seat of my car. "Different tactic this time huh?" he smirks.

"My car, my rules," I tell him. He grins and I grind on top of him. He hisses through his teeth and I kiss his neck. He groans and I slip my hands under his shirt. I pull it off of him and toss it in the front seat. He smirks at me and watches as I toy with him.

"Have I ever told you that you drive me wild?" he asks me. I shake my head no. "Well you do," he smirks. "All the time." He grabs me and flips us so I'm underneath him. I giggle and he kisses my neck down to my collar bone.

The next few hours are spent moaning and calling each other's names. I claw at Isaiah's back and find my release. Isaiah follows and we both lay in the back seat of my car sated and spent. Both of us breathing heavily. Isaiah holds me to him as we catch our breath. He kisses the top of my head lightly and I smile. I turn my head to look at him and he smiles down at me.

"You really wanna run?" he asks me.

I nod. "I'll get you and not have to keep it a secret all the time," I tell him with a smile.

"That you will, no sneaking around. I like the sound of that," he tells me. "Just you and me and the open road," he adds and stretches his hand out as he speaks.

"We would find some place to stay for a little while," I tell him. "We wouldn't constantly be driving."

"Yeah, I know," he says. He rubs my back softly. "Everything will be alright Claw," he reminds me. I lay my head on his chest and listen to the sound of his heartbeat. It's soft and steady. It lulls me to sleep again.

When I open my eyes again Isaiah is awake and looking at me. He smiles then kisses me. "Good morning," I say sleepily.

"More like afternoon," he replies with a slight laugh. "You've been asleep for a while. I didn't want to wake you. I know you have trouble sleeping."

Especially after dreams like that. Jeez I even have sleeping problems now.

"Thanks," I tell him. "I need to get going," I say. "Before Snake and Wolf come looking for me and you."

"Yeah, I had a good night last night. We leave day after tomorrow," he tells me. "And all worries of being caught are gone. Just me and you."

I nod, "I'll text you when I'm leaving Snakes place," I tell him. He nods and we climb into the front seat. He grabs my hand and intertwines our fingers over the center console. I smile a little at his gesture.

My internal battle grins and squeals. She is all girly girl. Completely opposite of me. Girly girl is not my thing and never has been.

"What?" he asks with a smile.

"You," I tell him.

"What about me?"

"Trying so hard at this relationship thing."

"And you're not?" he asks me. His voice angry. "I really want us to work so I will try as hard as I can to keep you. What about you Claw?" he asks me. "Are you not trying?" Now he seems hurt. I don't want to hurt him.

Gah! Don't question him!

"I'm trying, too Isaiah," I tell him. "I constantly think about you and what we would be doing if we were together. I'm asking you to run with me so we don't have to hide anymore. I want you and only you." And for the first time, I actually have my mind set. Nothing could replace Isaiah and the way he makes me feel. Nothing. Ever. Simple as that.

Hey, uh just so you know I win again! I give a half smile to my internal battle. I don't mind her winning right now.

"Claw, we can do this. And I'm willing to try hard at this than not at all," he tells me. He lifts my hand up to his lips and kisses my knuckles. "And I'm hoping you are too."

I stop my car next to his and turn it off. I look at him and grab his other hand. "Isaiah I love you," I tell him. "I've been trying since I said yes to you. And I'm still trying and always will be." I seal my words with a kiss.

He leaves his forehead on mine when our lips separate. "Claw," he starts. "What are you doing to me?" he whispers.

"Making you realize you've had me all along," I whisper back. He smiles at this. "And then some," I add with a smile of my own.

He pulls away from me and opens the car door. "I'll see ya soon," he says. "I love you."

All this love! And so much winning! My internal battle claps her hands and jumps up and down repeatedly.

"I'll see you soon and I love you, too," I tell him. He smiles and closes the door. I watch him walk to his car and get in. I wave at him and then drive to Snake's place.

The whole way there I think of me and Isaiah and our plan to run together. All it took was a simple explanation and he went with it. I'm glad he did. I couldn't leave him behind. I love him too much to leave him anywhere. He's trying at this relationship thing and I'm glad he is. He never seemed like much of a guy to try an actual relationship. And he said he could never lose me. I could never lose him. Once we leave we will become inseparable.

We'll travel out of state or a few counties away. Anywhere but this crap college town. Maybe to Summersville, Kentucky, which isn't too far from here. Or maybe we could travel to Tennessee or Illinois. Just away from here. Carla wouldn't find us. Snake, Wolf, and Momma Jeanine wouldn't find us. We would be all alone and better off.

Maybe not better off per say. I gape at her, negative bitch.

I park my car outside Snake's house and turn it off. I get out and walk inside. Nobody seems to be home. I walk inside and set my keys down in my room. I hear talking out back. I walk to the back door and listen. "She's been hangin' out with that Isaiah guy every night for the past four days," someone says.

Tell Isaiah! They'll find him!

"We'll stop her from seeing him," Snake says.

"Then we'll find Isaiah and take care of him," Wolf adds.

They know now! This plan you have to run needs to happen sooner rather than later. Staying here isn't gonna do any good for the two of you.

"You didn't hear it from me. I'm just telling you guys what I've seen." I'm trying to figure out who it is that's feeding them information.

"You know where they've been going?" Snake asks him.

"Some dead end road about four blocks from Cliff Point, Razor followed them one night," he says. *Damn it guy be quiet!* I think to myself. Damn Razor and those fraudulent college kids. I knew I shouldn't have trusted them. Even after I beat the shit out of them.

See? Violence does not solve problems!

"Alright, thanks Jack," Wolf says.

No! Jack is feeding them information? I hear them exchange a few more words then I hear the chairs move. "If you see Isaiah, Jack, tell him to watch his back," Wolf says with malice in his voice.

"Will do," he says then he's gone. I run to my room quickly and open the window. I sit in it and light a cigarette. Soon Snake and Wolf will be in here to interrogate me about Isaiah and my where abouts lately.

A few minutes pass and neither of them have come into my room. Maybe they don't know I'm home. That would be nice I could just stay in here all night and they would never bother me.

I put the cigarette out and let the wind blow through my hair. The seasons are changing which means my birthday is coming up. It's now early August. My birthday is late September. I wonder where I will be then. Who knows? Probably with Isaiah in another place.

Obviously with Isaiah, my internal battle rolls her eyes at me,

My door opens and Snake and Wolf come in. They close the door behind them. "If you're just gonna yell at me for being gone just save it," I tell them. "I'm almost nineteen I can do whatever the fuck I want."

"Who were you with?" Snake asks.

"No one," I reply. "I was alone. I always go to Cliff Point alone."

"You sure? Certain people have been seeing you with Isaiah," Wolf sneers.

"Well those certain people are wrong. I haven't been with anyone. Just myself," I tell them. "I don't know who you are getting your information from but obviously they're wrong."

"We have very trusted people to tell us what you're doing," Snake says. "The leader of Cliff Point needs to be watched or she could get hurt," he adds. His voice is angry yet threatening. He only uses that voice when someone needs a beating.

Oh mister tuff guy is coming out.

"Stop using that voice. You don't need to beat someone's ass," I tell him. "And I won't get hurt by anyone," I add. "I can care for myself."

"Claw, we know things about you. I've got trusted people who tell us everything," Snake tells me.

"You can attempt to hide this from us but it won't stay hidden long."

"And when we find Isaiah he will be good as dead when we're through with him," Wolf adds.

"Sure, that's if you can prove I've been going to see him," I scoff.

"We can Claw!" Snake shouts. "People have been coming to us after they see you two together. Goin' and seein' him multiple times a week. Sleeping with him in your car at the end of some dead end road down aways from Cliff Point."

"Word is gettin' out Claw. So just fucking tell us what's goin' on and then we'll leave you alone about the whole thing," Wolf adds.

Watch what you say Sheryl!

"Look, dip shits, ain't nothin' goin' on between me and Isaiah except sex. And here lately he just happened to be there when I go to Cliff Point. And me goin' to that dead end road is just so I can sleep. I go driving at night and end up there to sleep. By. Myself. Is that the answer you to were hoping for? Probably not but it's my side of the story and I'm sticking to it!"

Both of them sigh and leave my room slamming the door behind them. I let out a huge sigh. Thank goodness they left me alone.

And thank goodness yours and Isaiah's cover wasn't blown!

I find the eight cartons of Marlboro reds under my bed and stuff them in a duffle bag. I pack my clothes next. Day after tomorrow I will be heading somewhere with Isaiah and not looking back.

. . .

I wake up to an empty house. Snake, Wolf, and Momma Jeanine are gone to the store for the day. I told them not to bring me cause I don't do the whole shopping thing. I start taking my stuff to my car. Hair dye, smokes, and clothes are all in my car in less than twenty minutes. I text Isaiah and tell him I'm leaving Snakes and headed to the Old Country Store.

He replies that he's waiting for me in his car and all he will do is drive off behind me. Good. I don't have to wait for him to do anything except follow me.

I get in my car and start it. I drive to the Old Country Store and see Isaiah. I drive by and he pulls out behind me. He calls me and I answer my phone. "So babe, where we headed?" he asks me. My internal battle swoons at his name for me. She does that every time he says it. And I'm not gonna lie, I do too.

"I figured we would drive until we got tired then stop at a motel or something," I tell him. "Just kinda make it up as we go."

"Alright, sounds like a plan," he replies. "We'll discuss more later then, I'm assuming?" he asks me.

"Yep," I tell him.

"Okay, I'll just follow you then. Talk soon, love you," he says.

"Love you too, bye," I say and hang up my phone.

I drive for what feels like hours. I look at my phone and it has been hours. I call Isaiah, "the next exit we see we're stopping for the night and find some food."

"I was wondering when you would say that," I can hear the grin in his voice. "My stomach started to eat itself," he starts laughing.

"Well I'm getting' tired and hungry. And we've been on the road for about three hours. We need a break," I reply.

"Alright, next exit we'll stop."

"Alright, I love you."

"I love you more," he says and hangs up his phone.

I set my phone down and giggle uncontrollably. He said he loves me more. *Oh my gosh! Never in my wildest dreams! Isaiah loves you more than you can imagine!* I refrain from jumping up and down in my seat. I see an exit ramp up ahead and take that exit, turning left into a hotel parking lot.

We pull into the motel and get out of our cars. "Get a room first and order pizza?" he asks me. I nod. I'm exhausted from driving so long. We walk to the front desk hand in hand. The lady at the desk looks at us and smiles.

"Oh look at what we have here, a honeymoon couple?" she asks with a huge pearly white smile. She's all peppy smiles and blonde hair. Every bit the college freak who tries to impress her family.

"No ma'am, we just need a room for the night," I tell her. She glances up and down me and Isaiah both. She looks scared. Good.

"One bed?" she asks. "I'm just assuming," she adds quickly like we could hurt her if she says the wrong thing.

"Yeah," Isaiah replies rather coldly. I notice her look a little shocked at Isaiahs tone.

"How will you be paying?" she asks nervously.

"Cash," I say and put some money on the counter. She nods and takes the money from off the top of the counter.

"Alright, here is your room key. The number for Domino's pizza is on the back if you're hungry," she explains. "You two are room 212. Take a left out of the lobby door and it's the fifth door on the right."

"Thank you," I say. Isaiah grabs my hand and we walk out of the lobby. I lean my head on his shoulder as we walk. He smiles and looks for our room.

"Want me to carry you?" he asks me.

"Only if you want to," I tell him. Without warning he lifts me up and I squeal. "Isaiah!"

"What? I'm just carrying you," he says. "I won't drop you I promise," he adds then pretends to drop me and I squeal. He just laughs and continues walking.

I nod and wrap my arms around his neck. He stops in front of a door and opens it. He sets me on the bed and sits beside me. He pulls his phone out and orders a pizza for us to share. I crawl to the end of the bed and rest my chin on his shoulder. He smiles and looks at me out of the corner of his eye. "What are you thinking?" I ask him.

"About you," he says.

"What about me?" I ask him.

"How beautiful you are," he starts. "How much I love you and how now I don't have to hide the fact we're together and no one can stop us."

"Isaiah I'm so glad I have you," I whisper and kiss him.

"And I am glad I have you," he whispers. I fall back on the bed and Isaiah follows me. He pulls his shirt off and then mine. I giggle as he lands on top of me. We make out for a little while until there is a knock on our door.

"Damn," Isaiah swears under his breath.

"At least its food," I tell him.

"I'd rather have you," he smirks at me. I gasp and he answers the door. He comes back with pizza in hand and sets it on the bed. "But I think pizza will win out this time," he grins. I laugh and take a slice out of the box.

When we finish eating, Isaiah puts the rest of the pizza in the fridge and I take the rest of my clothes off and get under the sheets. Isaiah does the same and wraps his arms around me. "Good night Isaiah," I whisper.

"Good night, although it doesn't have to be yet," he says. "You are practically naked and I like that."

"Isaiah I'm tired, maybe in the morning," I tell him as I yawn.

Don't you think it's unusual that you're this tired? I shrug off my internal battle and stretch my limbs a little as I start falling asleep.

"Okay, go to sleep," he whispers. I nod and snuggle up to him. He kisses the top of my head and I drift off into a dreamless sleep.

Chapter 8

I'm standing in the motel room shower. I woke up about an hour ago. Isaiah is still asleep, however. I put my hands on the wall and rest my forehead on them as the water slides down my face and my back. It's refreshing but it allows me thinking time. I shouldn't be thinking but I am. If I start thinking I'll only think of the bad things that will come of this and not the good but here I go.

If we keep running will we ever stop? *No maybe not. You and he will be running for a long time if you keep this up!* I mean we have our whole lives ahead of us and here we are, running to stay together. I just want to be happy with him. And I want him to be happy with me. Is he happy with me? He acts like he is but I'm not sure. He says he's happy with me. *Sheryl he doesn't seem happy anymore. He says he's with you and loves you but is he sure?* I've fallen for him and hard, too. Too hard. *Way too hard! I didn't think you would fall this quickly! I blame you!* I wonder if he feels the same. *What if he doesn't? What will happen then?* And if we keep running will he feel the same later? All these questions running around in my head. I get frustrated with my internal battle and scream as I hit the shower wall.

And now your hand is going to hurt even worse! Stupid. I stamp my foot at her. My internal battle glares at me and get infuriated even more with her. Always arguing with me on these things when I have time to think.

I breathe in and out heavily until I calm down. I step out of the water and turn the shower off. "Shit," I swear under my breath when I realize I hit the wall with my injured hand. This could put a halt to things. Oh well. I step out of the shower and wrap a towel around my body. Careful not to bend my hand. I believe it's broken now. "Dammit," I huff and open the bathroom door. Isaiah is standing in the door way.

"You alright?" he asks me. He looks worried.

Maybe he does feel the same! My internal battle smiles and hugs herself.

"I heard you scream then a loud smack coming from the shower. What happened?"

"It's nothing," I lie. He doesn't need to know my doubts about this. *Yes he does!* "I just got a little frustrated about something and punched the wall." With my injured hand...

"Claw," he says sternly. "Tell me." I look up at him and he has a serious look on his face. Damn him and his looks.

A few minutes, silent minutes, pass when he speaks again. "Are you gonna tell me?" he demands. He does this a lot. Waits for me to tell him then asks twice. If I don't tell him he just stares at me until I do. Both of us keeping the silence.

It's me who speaks first. "No," I say like a child. And now I'm acting like a child. Why am I so afraid of him all of a sudden? I've never been afraid of anyone. Especially him. *Because you love him and are doubting whether he still loves you and is happy with you!*

"Why are you acting so small?" he asks me. His brow furrows and he lifts my chin gently with his thumb and index finger.

"I don't know," I say and pull my chin from his hold and look back at the floor. *Stop acting two!*

Isaiah lifts my chin again so I'm looking at him. "Claw everything will be alright," he tells me. "I'll keep you safe. Nobody can harm us now."

"I know that," I whisper. He pulls me to him and kisses my head. I hug him and squeeze him tightly and flinch when my hand throbs. He doesn't seem to notice when I do.

"I'm gonna shower," he tells me. I nod and let him go. He pulls his shirt off as he closes the door. I catch a glimpse of his shoulder and back muscles. Also the hint of the tattoo on his back. Just the slightest sight of him makes me swoon.

I change into some clothes and sit on the bed while Isaiah showers. I eat a slice of cold pizza left over from last night. I feel as if I've gotten weaker since I left Cliff Point. I'm not weak. I'm strong. I always have been strong. In my world you have to be strong. Not just for yourself but the people around you. There is no telling what could happen and when something does you have to push passed it like it never happened. It's what all of us do. Well manly Isaiah and myself do. Both of us come from troubled pasts that we'd like to forget ever happened.

Snake and Wolf are blowing my phone up asking where I am and who I'm with. I haven't answered them because they will come looking for me. Probably already are looking for me. It wouldn't surprise me. When the leader of Cliff Point goes missing it's something to freak out about.

I hear the bathroom door open and Isaiah strides out in just a towel. It hangs around his hips in an extremely hot way. A way that makes me swoon. Even my internal battle swoons at the sight of him in just a towel. One that makes me want to attack him and kiss every inch of his perfect V. He notices me starring and laughs a little. I blush and try to hide my face in embarrassment. I hear him walk over to me and he moves my hands. I flinch as he grabs my injured hand. He looks at me with concern.

"From when I punched the shower wall," I tell him. He nods and kisses the center of my palm.

"We should probably get it wrapped again," he tells me. I just nod. He grabs the wrap I took off of it and wraps it again. I thank him and he kisses me. A heated kiss that makes my insides melt. We inch our way up the bed to the head and we are all hands and kissing and touching. Oh I want him. But my internal battle from earlier resurfaces. *Does he still want you? Is he truly happy with you?*

I push on his chest, "Isaiah stop." My hand throbs as I push him. Although I didn't want to stop I have to know what he feels for me. How he honestly feels.

"What's wrong?" he asks me. His grey eyes search mine for some clue as to what I'm thinking. He sits up away from me. Several emotions flit across his face in a split second. He's so confusing to figure out.

I sit up and criss cross my legs. "How do you truly feel about me? And not just about me, how do you feel around me?" I ask him.

He grabs my uninjured hand and looks me in the eyes. "Claw, I love you. I'm happy when I'm with you. I like who I am when I'm with you. Before we slept together I used to watch you all the time. I would think *'God she's beautiful and one day I'll have her.'* Little did I know you were leader of Cliff Point." He rubs the back of his neck and looks at the bed. "And when we started sleeping together I thought I finally had you. And know that we are here, with each other, I'm the happiest I've ever been.

"Claw you make me happy. I want you and only you. I was wondering if you feel the same about me." He falls silent and takes a deep breath. He looks at our intertwined fingers then back at me. "I fell for you in a moment's notice when I first layed eyes on you. And now," he sighs again. Moment of truth. "I've fallen so deep for you, not even Snake or Wolf could change my mind about you. They could never keep me from you."

Awe! He feels the same about you! Hold on, I have to write this somewhere to remember for eternity.

I smile crosses my face and I launch myself at him. We both fall back on the bed laughing. "Oh Isaiah," I whisper. "I've never felt so happy in my life. I feel the same about you. I love you so much. So much it hurts." I kiss him on his lips and he kisses back. "Nobody could ever keep me from you. Not now. Not ever." He smiles and kisses me again.

. . .

It's late afternoon. We decided to stay another night in the motel so we could drive most of the day tomorrow. We haven't talked about a plan of action yet and we need to. Neither of us knows where we are going. All we know is that we are running so we can stay together.

Isaiah tried talking about it earlier but I stopped him because I just wanted to spend time with him. I didn't want to think about running or Snake and Wolf trying to find us or how this will all end up. I just wanted to spend time with him. This time is precious because neither of us knows how long we have before we are busted. And by busted I mean Snake and Wolf find us.

"Claw, we need a plan," Isaiah says to break the silence.

"I know," I sigh. "I've thought about it and we could stay in Summersville or go to a completely different state," I tell him. "It's just down to deciding where to stay."

"Let's try Summersville," he says. "Then what? Live in a motel or apartment or what?" he asks.

"We could find a cheap place to rent," I tell him. "One or both of us might have to get a job so we have money coming in. Because the money I have won't last long if we rent a place."

"True, we'll leave tomorrow morning. Find a place then look for a job," he says. "We could both work in a garage fixing cars. We're both good at it."

"Sounds like a plan," I reply.

"And I would love seeing you bent over the engine of a powerful car," he smirks and playfully slaps my behind.

"Oh Isaiah," I shake my head.

"What?"

"You never cease to amaze me. No matter the situation, you can always seem so playful."

"That's what I'm for," he grins at me.

"I'm glad." He nods and I lay next to him. He wraps his arms around me and pulls me close. I love the feeling of being pressed to his body. It brings me comfort and warmth. I sigh with content. Isaiah rubs my back softly. I listen to the rhythm of his heart as I begin to drift off to sleep.

.   .   .

We are driving to Summersville. We left early this morning after we both showered and ate breakfast at the diner across the street from the hotel. A quaint little place called Betty's.

We discussed more of our proposed plan. We will find a place to rent then find jobs. The money I had is dwindling away because of gas and food and the motel cost. I still have a good bit of it left but it goes fast. Around noon we pull into Summersville. I laugh at the corny sign they have when you cross the town limits.

Summersville, where it's always a warm, sun shiny day!

Sure it is. Especially since it's raining and a little cold out. Me and Isaiah park outside a McDonald's and go get some lunch.

We both order and eat in silence. Neither of us has ever been to Summersville before so we need to figure out our way around. It shouldn't be that hard. It's a small town. Only six hundred people according to the population count on the welcoming sign.

Which is probably wrong! I laugh at her statement. She's right, it is probably wrong.

Isaiah reaches across the table and grabs my hand. I smile at him. He smiles back and rubs his thumb across my hand. "I saw a sign for apartments for rent," he tells me.

"Did they look expensive?" I ask him as I sip my drink.

"No, but we'll have to go find out," he tells me. He's right. Appearances are deceiving. I nod and he throws our trash away. "You wanna go look at them? We have until five according to the sign."

"Yeah, we need to," I tell him. And we do. We can't stay in a motel for forever.

He nods and we both get up. We drive to the place where the apartments are for rent. It looks expensive. I hesitate as we walk up to the office.

"We will just talk to them," Isaiah tells me. "If it's too much we will find another place."

I nod and we walk in the office. We are seated immediately with someone who tells us all about the apartment complex and the great jobs close by. The good thing is these apartments aren't too expensive. Only $450 a month for a one bedroom apartment. I don't see why we would need two bedrooms we share a bed as it is. The renting agent takes us up to a one bedroom apartment and shows it to us.

"This one does have a half bath as well. It's not extra if you are wondering. Electricity and water bills are included in the $450 already. Any extra bills are on you not us," she explains. She's sweet. She's tall, blonde hair and bright blue eyes. All luscious lips and perky boobs. She looks like someone Snake would pounce on and have a one night stand with.

"Here is the master bedroom and master bath. The half bath is down the hall. All furniture and appliances are included already in this apartment. We want to make sure first time apartment owners don't worry about too much when they move in."

Isaiah has been holding my hand the whole time. Inspecting all the walls and flooring as we go. He makes sure everything is perfect.

Your knight in shining armor! Keeping you safe at all costs! My internal battle beams at me.

"Can me and my girlfriend look around for a minute or two alone?" he asks her.

"Of course, I'll be waiting in the lobby when you make up your mind," she says sweetly. "Oh and my name is Chelsea by the way."

"Okay, thank you," I say. She smiles and walks away. "So, what do you think?" I ask Isaiah apprehensively.

"I like the place. It's affordable and we already have the furniture we need. I looked at all the flooring and the wall structure. I just need to check the pipes," he says. I giggle a little. Isaiah always making sure everything is in order. I follow him to the kitchen then the bathroom and the half bath.

"And the prognosis is?" I giggle.

"It's in good shape," he replies. "Do you like it?" he asks. "I only want what makes you happy."

"I love it, but I want you to love it and be happy with it, too," I tell him.

He pulls me close to him and kisses the top of my head. "Claw, I love it and I'm happy with it. I'm happy with you. Now come on, let's go tell smiles a lot," he says. I smile and he kisses me softly. He grabs my hand and we walk to Chelsea's office.

"Made up our minds?" she asks us with a warm, welcoming smile.

"Yes, we have," Isaiah tells her as we sit down.

Chelsea nods and hands us some paperwork to fill out. It's a $450 dollar down payment on the apartment. I hand over the money and me and Isaiah sign the lease form. Chelsea takes us back up to the apartment with two sets of keys.

"These are the only keys you get. Each set has a key to unlock the garage gate for your cars. No guests allowed and you may have pets if you wish. The pets cannot be loud and must be kept inside," she informs us. Me and Isaiah both nod. "Have a fantastic day and I hope you enjoy your new home!" she exclaims and clasps her hands together. "Also, if the lease needs to be terminated, you can terminate it. It doesn't take long all we need is the last months' rent and for you to sign the form to get out of the apartment."

Chelsea walks off and Isaiah unlocks the door to our apartment. He picks me up and carries me inside. I giggle and kiss his cheek. He sets me down and we look around some more. The kitchen has a stove, oven, microwave, dishwasher, and a coffee maker. Although we have no use for a coffee maker. The living room has a couch and an extra chair with a coffee table. The bed room has a bed, two dressers, and a huge closet. The bathroom has a shower, bath tub, and closet as well. We got lucky with this one. All there is to buy is bed sheets, towels, and food.

Isaiah walks up behind me and hugs me from behind. "Home sweet home," he whispers as he kisses my neck. "Let's go get our stuff," he says and releases me.

We walk downstairs to our cars and get our belongings. I hope they don't have a smoking rule since both me and Isaiah smoke. Isaiah carries my things along with his up to the apartment. He sets the duffle bags on the bed and I sit beside them. Isaiah walks over to me and kneels in front of me. "What is it babe?" he asks me.

"We got really lucky with this apartment Isaiah," I tell him. "I'm glad we found this place."

"We did, and I'm glad we found it, too," he says. "But there's something more, isn't there?"

"It's nothing."

"Tell me," he demands. He's not to be argued with.

"Isaiah I feel like we've gotten too lucky." My internal battle shakes her head at me and sighs.

"How?"

"Something bad always follows me with getting lucky," I explain. "I can feel it." *Shut your face! Not all the time!*

Isaiah sighs, "We'll be fine. Besides, we need to go shopping though. And I know you don't like to shop but we need to."

"I know we do. We need bed sheets and towels and food," I say. He nods. "And we need to look for jobs so we have money coming in."

"I know, but first lets go get what we need," he says. I nod and get up.

We take my car to the nearest super market that could have all your possible needs. My car is bigger than Isaiah's car so we can fit more in the trunk and back seat.

I get bored with in five minutes of being there. Even my internal battle is bored out of her mind. Isaiah starts acting goofy so I'll at least smile. Neither of us bothered to make a list of things we need so if we forget something oh well. We'll get it later. We get bed sheets and towels first then food.

As we walk down the food aisles, Isaiah just starts throwing things in the grocery cart. I laugh at him and start putting it back on the shelf as I walk. "Isaiah, we can't buy one of everything," I laugh at him.

"Finally a laugh!" he exclaims and laughs. "I was only doing it so you would laugh," he explains and kisses my cheek. He drapes an arm over my shoulders as we walk through the aisle. He is every bit the nonchalant guy with his crooked grin and his eyes bright with humor.

"Well now that I'm laughing we need to get serious on things we need," I tell him. He nods in agreement and we continue on our way. We get to the cash register and the cashier looks at us funny. "We just got an apartment," I tell her.

She nods, "first time in a place together on your own?" she asks us. We both nod. "I hope ya like it. And have fun but don't be late on ya rent," she tells us.

Isaiah and I both nod. She doesn't know us from Adams house cat and she talks like she knows us. I guess that's how everyone is in this town. I guess we'll get used to it. And if I don't I have Isaiah to talk to and keep me company.

Isaiah carries the heavier stuff to the apartment. Like the food and laundry detergent and other stuff. I carry the lighter of our groceries because he told me not to worry about it and that I shouldn't hurt myself. I've carried heavy stuff all the time. It's never bothered me none and why would it now? I hope he doesn't see me as weak or something. Just because I ran from Louisville doesn't make me weak. I hated it there so I left. And Isaiah hated it there, too.

I make the bed and put the towels in the bathroom while Isaiah puts everything else away. I walk into the kitchen and smell something cooking. And it smells delicious. I intend to ask him if he sees me as a weakling because we ran from Louisville. But right now I just want to eat what he cooked.

"Smell good?" he asks me.

"Very much so," I say and take a big whiff of the air.

"It's homemade soup," he explains. "Something simple for our first night in our new apartment," he explains. "I figured I would go ahead and cook dinner since you were busy," he adds. He kisses me softly and hugs me to him.

"That was sweet of you," I reply. "Is it ready yet? I'm starving."

"Yeah, it's ready. I was waiting on you," he says. I nod and we sit down to eat.

The soup tastes as good as it smells. I eat two bowls of it and I'm full. Isaiah can cook. Who would have ever thought that he could cook?

"Living on my own, you learn the basics of cooking," he tells me, reading my thoughts.

I glance at him and nod my head.

After we eat I clean the dishes and put them away. I hear the shower running when I walk into the bedroom. I start putting my clothes away while Isaiah showers. I start thinking about what I thought about earlier. Does Isaiah think I'm weak? I'm not weak. I moved away from a problem. A problem I've been dealing with since I was thirteen.

He does not see you as weak Sheryl. Or does he? I'm confused...

I hear the shower turn off and Isaiah walks out of the bathroom in a towel. He grins when he sees me sitting in the middle of the bed. He strides over to me and kisses me softly. I smile when he pulls away. He walks over to one of the dressers and pulls out underwear and sleep pants. I watch as his muscles move with his muscle movements. His dragon tattoo moves and it looks like it could fly off his back and fly around the room.

Isaiah is strong. Stronger than me. Possibly stronger than I will ever be. Maybe I am weak. But to be the leader of Cliff Point you have to be strong. I guess I was only pretending. As I watch Isaiah move around the bedroom I can't help but think that being with him made me stronger. He has never acted as if I'm weak. He tells me I'm strong all the time. But the problem is do I believe him? I don't see myself as strong anymore.

Now that I've left Cliff Point, I don't feel the need to be strong and mean. But I still have that fire I need to be that way.

Isaiah sits on the bed next to me and kisses my bare shoulder. I'm only in a bra and grey sweat pants. "Your birthday is coming up," he whispers as he kisses up to my ear.

"I know," I sigh. I don't like my birthday. Too many soiled birthday attempts by Carla and Frank.

"What do you want?" he asks me then kisses the sensitive spot behind my ear.

"You," I moan. I grip the sheets tightly.

"You've got me, and I'm not talking about right now," he grins and kisses that spot again. "What do you want for your birthday?" he asks me.

"I've got all I could ever want," I tell him. He smiles and kisses my lips. He takes my bottom lip between his teeth and tugs. Electricity courses through my body igniting my blood. Oh what he does to me. I turn to face him. I wrap my arms round his neck and fist my hands in his hair.

"There's gotta be somethin' you want," he whispers against my lips.

"I've got you. There's nothin' else I want." He caresses the side of my face. His thumb running over my cheek bone. "Right now, the apartment and you," I pause for a second and smile. "It's somethin' to celebrate over."

"Let's celebrate then, shall we," he whispers.

"Yes," I moan as he caresses me. I fall back on the bed and Isaiah follows. Soon we are both lost in sheets and skin. Touches and kisses and hands everywhere. It is then I realize how broken we both are. Both of us come from broken families and we are two people lost, tragically, in the middle.

I hold onto Isaiah in the after math of our celebration. Both of us breathing heavily. I feel something wet fall onto my chest. I look at Isaiah and realize he's crying. My strong Isaiah. He's realized it, too. Isaiah moves and lays beside me. He faces away from me. Probably so I won't see him cry. Nobody has ever seen him cry. And that's because Isaiah doesn't cry. I sit up and lean over him. I rub his arm gently. "Isaiah, what's wrong?" I ask. Although I think I know what it is.

You know what's wrong! I glare at her, snarky bitch.

"I just realized something," he says. He rubs his eyes and looks at me. Eyes red and puffy. Oh Isaiah. My heart constricts.

"What is that?" I ask as I look into his sorrow filled eyes.

"We are both broken," he whispers. "Broken people lost in the middle of our broken families. And it just hit me."

"I realized the same thing," I reply. I rest my chin on his arm. We both sigh. Isaiah wraps an arm around me and looks into my eyes. I run my fingers through his hair and he smiles a small smile.

"Claw, are we doing the right thing?" he asks me. I look at him puzzled. "I mean, running from our past. Shouldn't we embrace it?" he asks me.

"I don't know about you but I've tried to embrace it. Many times. I always ended up hurt by it," I explain.

"I've tried before, too," he tells me. "The past always hurts. No matter how much we try to change it."

"You can't change the past but you can change the future," I tell him. "You can always change the course of your future. It may be a difficult challenge but it's always worth it in the end."

"I knew there was a reason I fell in love with you," he smiles and kisses me. "This ass is still mine though," he adds as he squeezes my behind. "Nobody else's," he warns.

"Yeah, yeah," I reply. "I know and stay clothed."

"Oh baby you don't have to stay clothed any more. It's just me and you here. You can bare it all," he smirks at me.

"Keep your pants on," I say and slap his chest playfully.

"That's hard to do around you," he says and bites my shoulder. I squeal and he hovers over me. I wrap my arms around his neck and kiss him.

I'm here with the one guy I truly have ever loved. My broken boy. I love him so and he loves me even if I'm broken like he is.

He lays beside me again and I yawn. "I love you," I whisper.

"I love you," he whispers back. He pulls me to him and I snuggle up closer.

I am with Isaiah and I don't have to hide it anymore. Neither of us has to hide anymore. We can be together without the fear of Snake and Wolf coming after us. Me and Isaiah are where we want to be. And we are both happy. And that is all that matters.

Chapter 9

Isaiah and I have gotten a job working for the same garage about a half mile from the apartment. Which I am doing easy work because of my hand. I fractured it after punching the wall in the hotel room last week. I guess it's what I get for fighting with my internal self. Anyway, it's easy money for the two of us so maybe we won't have to dig into my saved money. It's gone from $500,000 to around $450,000. With gas and the hotels and food and from moving into the apartment, it's dwindling away and we have to keep money somehow.

The other good part about all of this is if we need to up and leave in a moment's notice we can. Me and Isaiah are only working part time and the apartment lease is easy to get out of. This is great because Snake sent me a message yesterday that disturbed me. One that I wish I had never opened and read. I haven't shown it to Isaiah yet. And I should, he shouldn't be kept in the dark about anything Snake wants to do to him but I can't tell him.

"I've heard word that you are staying in a town close by. Keep an eye on that boy of yours. It'll be the end of him before you know it," that's what the message read.

And since I got it I have followed Isaiah pretty much everywhere. I can't let him get hurt or killed by Snake and Wolf and whomever they have on their side.

"Sheryl!" I hear my name being called. I get up and follow a nurse down a corridor. She walks into a room and I follow. "The doctor will be in shortly," she tells me and closes the door as she leaves.

I haven't been feeling well lately. I wake up feeling nauseous and a few times I've actually thrown up. Sometimes I can't even keep food down.

I swing my legs back and forth as they dangle off the edge of the exam table. It's deathly quiet in this exam room. The door opens, startling me, and a lady in a white coat and navy blue scrubs walks in.

"Hello, I'm Dr. Mitchum," she introduces herself. "Now, tell me what your symptoms are?"

"Nausea, vomiting. I can't keep most food down," I tell her.

"Alright, I don't think it's the flu or anything serious. But I am, however, going to run tests for various things," she explains. I nod. She swabs my nose and throat, "For bacterial infections," she says. Then hands me a clear cup.

I give her a quizzical look. "One other test," she says. I blanch. "By the look on your face and how fast your face turned pale, you know what test the cup is for."

"Yeah," I say tight lipped.

"I'm still going to run the other tests but from the few symptoms you gave me, the only thing that this could be is you're pregnant. But I won't know for sure until I run the tests," she tells me. "Leave the sample in the bathroom, and then come back. I want to ask one more question."

I nod and walk down the hall to the rest room. Holly fuck! Me pregnant? No! *It's possible Sheryl. You and Isaiah had a little mishap a while back!* My internal battle reminds me. Shit!

I leave the sample in the rest room like I was told and walk back into the exam room. Dr. Mitchum looks at me and smiles warmly. "I have one question," she starts. "The results will take a while to come back and the RN informed me you are short on time. I can have the office send you the results via text message if you would like. I'm only doing this for you because I've seen plenty of girls come through my office in the same situation you're in. However, yours seems worse off than what I've seen."

I nod my head, "Alright, thank you." She nods and hands me something. "What's this for?" I ask quietly.

"On the off chance I'm correct, take one tablet every day," she tells me. "This is the last time I will see you. You're on the move. I'm sure you'll see various doctors about this on the way. I'm just getting you started. And think long and hard when we send the test results."

"Okay, I will," I say quietly. She smiles a small smile and dismisses me.

As I drive back to the apartment all I do is worry about what the results will be. *You'll be fine whatever the results may be. Don't worry too much. Isaiah will notice and ask about it!* This time I actually agree with her. Isaiah will ask what I'm so worried about. And then all will be spilled.

Isaiah is at work today while I'm stuck in the apartment. I guess they don't have a non-smoking rule because we haven't gotten in trouble yet. As far as trouble goes, however, if Snake finds us we will be in trouble.

Carla texted me a few days after we left. Snake told her Isaiah and I ran and she asked me about it. However, I didn't reply because she doesn't need to know my business. She sent me this long drawn out message about the mistake I'm making and how Snake is looking for me and how much she misses me. All her sappy bull shit to get me to come home. It never works and never will work because I hate her.

Even I hate her.

"Such fucking bull shit," I say under my breath as I let out a cloud of smoke. I put out my cigarette and walk back in the apartment. I look at the clock, Isaiah should be home soon. It's near four o'clock. Maybe I should tell him about the message, but how? And when? Maybe right as he comes home? No, that would ruin his joy when he sees me. While we're having sex? No, that could go bad and one or both of us could get hurt. Maybe…maybe… shit I don't know when. I'll just tell him. Just when ever. I'll let it come out like word vomit.

Fast and all at once. Yeah, I'll do that. It would be quick and pain less that way.

I hear the door open and Isaiah strides over to me. "Hey babe," he says and kisses me. I wrap my arms around his neck and kiss him back. "Somethin's wrong isn't it?" he asks when he pulls away.

"No…yes…maybe," I stutter. Shit how does he know something is wrong? *Because he loves you and cares about you!*

"What is it?" he asks me, more demanding this time.

Here it goes, just do it fast and all at once. Word vomit. "Snake is looking for us and he texted me yesterday saying so and he's gonna…gonna…" I can't speak the last word. It's too painful to say.

"He's gonna what Claw? Tell me what's he gonna do?" Isaiah demands. He places his grease covered hands on both sides of my face and looks deep into my eyes.

"Kill you," I whisper almost to myself. My eyes grow wide with panic. I grip Isaiah's arms tighter and feel tears pool in my eyes. Isaiah gone. Dead even when Snake finds him. I can't lose him. He means so much to me. I look up into Isaiah's eyes and he stares back, grey eyes with a burning intensity that lets me know he'll be fine.

"Claw, I'll be okay. If he comes close to us we'll run again. We'll be okay," he tells me. I can hear the softness in his voice. It's just a little raspy, but I know we'll be okay for now. He pulls me to him and I take a deep breath. I breathe in the smell of motor oil and gasoline on his work shirt. "Let's go shower," he whispers. I nod and he grabs my hand and leads me down the hall to our room.

I sit on the bed only in shorts and a tank top. Isaiah wraps my hand after he puts something on it. For someone so tough and hard he knows how to use a gentle touch. Deft fingers work on my hand so he won't hurt me. He kisses me gently then walks back into the bathroom so he can shave. He hates having facial hair so he shaves daily. I don't mind the stubble on his chin though; it tickles when he kisses me. I walk out of our bedroom to the kitchen and grab something to drink for me and Isaiah. When I walk into our room he looks confused.

"What is it?" I ask him. I set the drinks down and walk over to the bathroom door. He has my phone in his hands.

"Your phone was on the counter. It went off so I looked at it," he explains. Which I don't mind, I have nothing to hide from him. He lets me go through his phone and he goes through mine.

"Yeah, and?" I say. Wait; there was something I was trying to hide from him. Something I didn't want him to see. "Isaiah give me my phone," I say and snatch it from him. He grabs at my phone to get it back but I run from him.

"Claw what test?" he asks me sternly. Although his voice radiates confusion.

"It's nothing Isaiah. Don't worry about it," I tell him. He goes to grab my phone again but I jump to the other side of the bed away from him.

"Claw whatever it is it came back positive," he says. "Give me your phone."

"Isaiah, I didn't want you to find out," I say, panic laced through my voice. *Oh my God!* My internal battle is screaming at me and jumping for all she's worth. I'm pregnant.

"Claw, me and you, we don't keep secrets. Give me the damn phone," he says and walks over to me. He's angry. "Just fucking tell me or let me see the phone!" he hollers at me.

I clutch my phone to my body. He can't know. He can't. "No Isaiah," I say quieter. "Not this time."

Isaiah stops in front of me. He puts his hands down by his sides and stares at me. Then he looks at the floor and speaks. "I saw something else while I was looking at your phone," he tells me and runs a hand through his hair.

"What?"

"Snake is coming to Summersville. We have to go. Now," he explains. "We have until sunrise. I already told Dave at the garage we are leaving and I got us out of the lease."

Jeez he works fast.

"Isaiah," I whisper and slide down the wall to the floor. I bury my face in my hands and begin to sob. Damn why am I crying so much? Oh right. I know why.

"Claw," he says and picks me up. He sits on the bed with me in his lap. "Everything will be okay. We'll be gone by the time Snake and his guys get here," he tells me. "Oh and one more thing," he says.

"Yeah?"

"I sold my car."

"What?" I sit back and look at him with shock. "Why would you do that Isaiah? You love your car. Why would you sell it?"

"Your money won't last us forever. We only have $450,000 left of it. And I got $80,000 for my car. Paid in full by the guy who bought it. It's just a car babe, we have yours. And with one car we won't have to spend as much money on gas," he explains. "We have $530,000. We will be okay for a while."

"Isaiah, are we really gonna keep running?" I ask him. With me being pregnant it's not such a good idea anymore.

"Yes, yes we are. If that's what it takes to keep us safe."

I wrap my arms around his neck and kiss his neck gently. He wraps his arms around me and sighs heavily. "What about all this?" I ask him.

"Only our clothes go with us. Everything else stays," he says. "Except maybe blankets. Take those," he adds. I nod and bury my face in his neck. He rubs my back softly. I love being in his arms. I feel safe and at home with him. But with the news I have, who knows what he will think or do.

Neither of us sleeps that night. Both of us packing and taking everything to my car. It's getting colder out. Which in Kentucky it's usually cooler at night. But since the seasons are changing the temperature drops even more. Isaiah notices me shivering and puts his jacket around my shoulders. He kisses my temple and I smile. He smiles back and walks back into the apartment. We've only been here a week and a half and now we have to leave. It sucks but we can't let Snake get to us.

"Alright, that's the last of it," Isaiah says as he closes the trunk of my car. "Let's go." I nod and get in my car. It's almost three in the morning. Snake might pass us on the highway but maybe we will be long gone by the time he starts heading this way.

"Where are we going Isaiah?" I ask him as I pull out onto the open road.

"Just drive babe," he says. "When we get tired we'll pull into a motel somewhere." I nod and just drive. I don't know where we will go or if we will ever stop running. But that's what we've always done. Run from our pasts because we can't face them. I know it's not the best thing to do but we are all we have. Just me and him.

. . .

Day one of being on the road. It's going good I guess. Isaiah drives when I'm too tired to. No trouble so far. I've gotten one text from Snake asking where we are and if I don't say then he will keep looking for us. Figures.

We are pulling into a hotel after driving for eight and half hours. Isaiah pays for a room and comes and gets me out of the car. I'm exhausted from lack of sleep last night and most of the day. He picks me up and carries me to our room. I wrap my arms around his neck and lean my head on his shoulder. He kisses my forehead and I smile a little.

Isaiah stops walking and opens a door. A few moments later he sets me down on a bed. "Go to sleep Claw," he whispers and kisses me softly.

"Don't leave," I say with my eyes closed. I grab his arm so he can't leave. "Please."

"I'll be right back. I'm gonna get our stuff," he explains. "I'll be okay," he whispers and kisses me softly. And with that I let go of his arm and he's gone.

I drift off to sleep not long after Isaiah returns. He pulls me to him and I hold onto him. Soon he won't be able to. That's if he stays when I tell him. I have no clue how he will take it when I do tell him. I want to tell him but I don't know how. It's so frustrating trying to know when to tell him. I should be able to just tell him. He'll figure out eventually what the test was positive about. Either he'll look at me and be able to tell or he'll see I'm thinking about something and demand to know what's wrong. Either way he will find out eventually.

. . .

Day four. We've been driving for three days. Snake hasn't texted me in a while. Maybe he's just given up on trying to find us. Isaiah doubts he has but it brings me peace to think he has given up. That first day in the hotel room brought my internal battle to a whole new level. I'm starting to become antsy and nervous. Isaiah hasn't noticed and if he has he hasn't said anything about it. I really want to tell him.

Sheryl, just. Tell. Him. Please! My internal battle begs me.

"Isaiah," I whisper. We are pulled over on the side of the road to rest for a few hours.

"Yeah?"

"I'm cold," I shiver.

"Come here," he says and wraps his arms around me. He pulls the blanket up over me and I snuggle up closer to him. "Better?" he asks.

"Much," I reply. I drift off into a dreamless sleep.

When I wake my car is moving. Day five on the road. "Good morning sleepy head," Isaiah smiles at me.

"Good morning," I reply and sit up. "How long have you been driving?"

"About an hour. You were sleeping so peacefully I figured I would drive while you slept," he explains.

"Oh, thanks." I push the blanket off of me and climb in the front seat. Isaiah grabs my hand and kisses my knuckles. I giggle a little because his stubble tickles my hand. He rubs his thumb over my hand as he drives. He is so sweet sometimes but others he can be kinda mean. Never towards me but to others.

Isaiah drives for another few hours until we stop for lunch. I fell back asleep until Isaiah woke me up to tell me where we are. "I'll drive now," I tell him.

"You sure? You've been sleeping a lot lately," he says.

"Yeah, I'm sure," I tell him. "You drove all morning so I'll drive all afternoon until I get tired then we'll stop at a hotel or somethin'."

Isaiah nods. "Okay, sounds like a plan."

After lunch I drive off down the road. About an hour into driving Isaiah falls asleep. I know he's asleep when he starts snoring. I giggle a little. I keep my eyes on the road. We have driven all around Kentucky. Visiting every place there is. Historic or not we have seen it so far. Soon we will have to leave Kentucky and go to another state so Snake and Wolf won't find us. But for now we will be okay. The three of us.

I place a hand on my belly and choke back a sob. I'm only eighteen and I'm pregnant. I wipe the tears from my eyes and let out a shuttering sigh. I'm roughly two months along. That's what the message on my phone was. The doctor told me she would text me the results and only say if the test was positive or negative but not for what because I know Isaiah would look through my phone. I want to tell him but I just can't find the nerve to tell him.

You're killing me here. Would you please tell him?! I shake my head at her. I can't. I don't have the nerve to tell him.

"How am I gonna tell your daddy?" I ask as I run my thumb over my stomach. I see a tear fall on my shirt and I quickly look back up at the road. There is no traffic out what so ever. It's beginning to rain and it's getting dark out. I see an exit sign that has multiple lodging places and I take the exit ramp. I turn left at the red light and head towards a Motel 6. I nudge Isaiah awake. "Isaiah, wake up."

"I'm up," he says and wipes his eyes. "Where are we?"

"A motel," I reply. "It's almost six and I'm getting tired. Come on," I say. He nods and gets out of the car.

"I'll get our stuff if you'll go pay for the room," he says. I nod and walk to the front desk.

I'm greeted by a brunette woman. Tall and thin with brown eyes smacking away on her gum. "How may I help you?" she says as she smacks. Racking on my nerves, that bitch is.

"Can I get a room with one bed?" I ask her.

"We only have two bed rooms available at the moment," she retorts. My anger rises and I hold back from ripping her head off.

"Then can I get one of those?" I ask her getting agitated.

"Yeah, I guess," she says. "How long will you be staying?"

"Just tonight. Me and my boyfriend are just passing through," I explain.

"Alright, sixty-eight dollars please," she tells me. I hand over the money and she hands me the room key. "Here, four rooms down."

I walk outside to see Isaiah standing next to my car with our stuff. "Come on," I say and take my bag from him. He grabs my hand and we walk to our room. I open the door and set my stuff on the floor.

Isaiah sets his stuff down and grabs my from behind. "You okay?" he asks then kisses my neck. I nod and let out a moan. "Don't hide from me. Your eyes are red and puffy like you've been crying," he replies.

"I'm just scared." *Scared of how you'll react to my baby news.*

"Of what? We're safe right now," he tells me. He picks me up and sets me on the bed then hovers over me. He kisses all over my neck and chest and I moan and grip the sheets. "Tell me what you're scared of," he says.

"It's nothing Isaiah," I tell him. My internal battle shakes her head at me.

"Come on tell me," he says. He continues to kiss all over me. He pulls my shirt off and kisses down to my stomach. I stiffen when he kisses my stomach. He looks up at me concerned. "Claw, what's wrong?" he asks me. I look down at him and begin to cry again. "Shit," he swears under his breath. He crawls back up to me and kisses my nose. "Will you please tell me what is wrong? Please."

I let out a shuttering sigh and wipe my eyes. "It has to do with what you saw five days ago," I tell him.

"The positive thing?" he asks me. I nod and sniffle. "What was it positive for?"

Well here it goes. "Isaiah," I pause. "I'm pregnant." My internal battle jumps up and shouts but stops as I see Isaiah's face change.

Chapter 10

"You're what?" His eyes wide with fear. My hopes for him to accept this plummet far below where I want them to be.

"I'm pregnant," I repeat. I get out from underneath him and walk across the hotel room. I begin to cry again. He's going to leave I know he is. I don't think he ever wanted kids or a family, really. And I've just told him I'm pregnant.

"How far along?" he asks. His voice tense, strained to hide his emotion.

I can't look at him. His facial expression burns through me and I know he's upset. Not the sad upset but angry or confused. "Two months," I reply with a small sob.

I hear Isaiah's heavy footsteps pace behind me. What is he going to do? I don't want him to leave. He can't leave me alone or go back to Cliff Point. Snake and Wolf will kill him if and when he returns and that will devastate me. I wipe the tears away that are rolling down my cheeks. "So that's what the message was for? The doctor sent you a text saying the test came back positive?"

"Yes," I reply smally. "I wanted to tell you sooner but I couldn't because I didn't know how you would take it. I knew you would find out eventually but I didn't know how to tell you," I explain to him. Fear wrenching deep in my gut the longer this conversation lasts. My internal battle remains quiet, she knows this is not the time to put her two cents in.

It stays silent for a few minutes. Long minutes. I hear Isaiah sit on the edge of the bed and let out a long drawn out sigh. I glance at him through the mirror on the wall above the sink in the room. He's looking at me with his thinking look. I look back down at my feet and sniffle and cover my face with my hands. He's going to leave I know he is. He never stays silent this long. I start to sob even louder the more I imagine him walking out on me.

I can see him just walking out of this room. Leaving me and our unborn child alone. There is no telling where he'll go. I can hear the echo of his footsteps walking away. It seems so real. My legs go numb and I collapse to the floor sobbing uncontrollably. Huge sobs racking my body at just the thought of him leaving me.

We never intended for this to happen. We used protection and never had sex when it was my time of the month. *The one uh oh a while back!* I ignore her. I didn't think anything of that when it happened.

But I can't do anything to an innocent child. And the thought of something happening to it makes me hurt inside. The thought of Isaiah leaving hurts.

"Shh, it's okay," I hear Isaiah's soft voice tell me. "Hush now," he whispers. He picks me up off the floor and sits on the bed with me in his lap. He rubs my back softly and kisses my forehead gently. He's taking this surprisingly better than I thought he would.

"You're not m-mad at me?" I ask, choking back a sob.

"No, I'm not mad. It just happens," he tells me. "Yeah it would have been ideal to wait for something like this. Like when we aren't on the run from a psychotic group of guys wanting to kill us. But I'm not mad."

"I'm sorry," I tell him.

"You don't have to be sorry," he tells me. "I have just as much to do with this as you. Why are you sorry?"

I shrug and wrap my arms around his neck and lean my head on his shoulder. He's already accepted the fact he's going to be a father. We're only eighteen and we're going to be parents. Shit. Our lives just got harder.

And you think of that now?! Your lives got harder when the doctor sent the message!

I kiss his neck gently and shift so my legs are on either side of him. He rubs my back as I continue to kiss his neck. He lets out a soft sigh. I nibble at his neck and he moans. He starts kissing my neck and I moan in response. My body is extremely sensitive. Twice as much blood pumping through me because of the baby. I reach my hands up to his hair and tug.

"Sensitive are we?" he smirks.

"Oh, you have no idea," I say as I sigh. He grins and kisses the sweet spot behind my ear. I practically come apart. I start to move on his lap as his hands skim my body. I throw my head back and he kisses every inch of my throat. I claw at his back.

Isaiah lays me back on the bed and hovers over me. I pull his shirt off and toss it across the room. I work on his pants next and slide them off with my feet. Isaiah flips us so I'm on top of him. He slowly pulls my jeans off. His hands skim over my lace thong and it sends shivers through my body. He does it once more and I come apart at the seams. Shouting his name. He holds me to him as I come back to earth. "Did you really just-"

"Yeah, I did," I interrupt him.

"Alright," he says and claims me once more.

I wake up in the passenger seat of my car. Trees and bushes flying past the window. I feel something touching my stomach. I look down to see Isaiah's hand there. His thumb rubbing softly back and forth in a slow motion. "Isaiah," I say quickly.

"Yeah?" he asks me.

"Pull over, I need to vomit," I say. He does as I say and pulls over. I throw the door open and lean out of the car. I feel his hand rub my back as I vomit all over the side of the highway. I finish vomiting and close the door. I wipe my face off and lean back in the seat.

"You okay?" he asks me.

"I'm fine, that is part of this for the first three months," I explain. He nods and pulls back onto the highway.

Day six on the open road. So far no accidents except the fact that I'm pregnant. Which both of us accept it. Isaiah puts his hand back where it was and I smile a little.

I see a sign that reads:

Thanks for staying in Kentucky!

Come back soon!

I guess we've gone everywhere in Kentucky we can go. Now it's time to head out of state. That would be better than staying in Kentucky where Snake can easily find us. The three of us will be safe once we get out.

Isaiah drives for another hour when I start to get hungry. He pulls into a Dairy Queen so we can eat. "I'll drive if you want me to," I tell him.

"Nah, I'll drive. I have a place for us to stay in mind," he tells me. "It's in Tennessee."

"Oh," I say. This is news. *Why didn't he say before?*

"You'll love it, and besides we might stay there longer than you think. We could stay safe." I like the idea of us being safe. "Me, you, and our little one," he adds. I smile and feel a stray tear roll down my cheek. I look over at Isaiah who is smiling too. He puts his hand on my stomach and smiles even bigger.

We leave Dairy Queen and Isaiah drives. It'll still be another day or two before we get there. We've only just gotten out of Kentucky and the traffic is bad. And according to Isaiah the place we are staying at is almost in Alabama. It's close to the Tennessee-Alabama state line. I don't mind though. As long as we are safe and away from Snake and his plans to kill Isaiah.

I fall asleep as Isaiah drives. I start to dream.

Me and Isaiah are in Tennessee. I look roughly six months pregnant. Where ever we are it seems peaceful. I sigh with content. Isaiah smiles at me and rubs my swollen belly. I smile even more. We are inside a nice warm, cozy house. It feels like home.

Isaiah begins to speak and then all of a sudden the room goes dark. I can't hear him. He becomes distant from me but he's not walking. He's kneeling in front of me holding my hand. I scream for him but he doesn't hear me. I scream again but he still doesn't hear me. The light comes back but Isaiah is gone. I look down at my belly but it's flat. I scratch my head. Where's the baby? I hear crying and run to where it's coming from. I see a crib. I run to it but I run into a glass wall. I see someone picking up my baby. I scream for them to put him or her down but they can't hear me. I bang on the wall with my fist and the person doesn't turn around.

Who is this mysterious person? And why can't I hold my baby? Where is Isaiah? All these questions running through my mind. The person finally moves and I see Isaiah sitting in a chair. He's crying. Why is he crying? I get a good look at the mysterious person. It's a nurse. She's medium height with black hair. She hands the baby to Isaiah and his eyes light up even through the tears rolling down his cheeks. Then all the words come running from the nurse's mouth. The glass wall evaporates like it was never there before. "I'm sorry sir but your girlfriend didn't make it. This happens sometimes in child birth. I am very sorry," she says softly and walks away. I run to Isaiah and yell at him.

"Isaiah I'm right here! I'm not dead look at me!" I yell. He doesn't look though. He can't hear me. I walk around him and look down at our baby. She's precious. She looks just like me except she has Isaiah's eyes and hair. I start to cry. I'm never going to get to see her. She'll never know me. "No!" I scream and cry harder. "Isaiah please look at me! I'm still here! Please!" I yell. I wrap my arms around him but he only looks at our daughter.

"If only your mommy was here to see you," he sobs. "You look just like her."

"Isaiah I'm right here!" I shout at him. "Answer me! Please!"

"Claw wake up," I hear someone tell me. "Babe wake up please." It's Isaiah. He starts nudging me and I jump awake. "You're okay. I can see you sitting there," he tells me.

I look around and my car is parked on a back road. I'm breathing heavily and I'm sure my eyes are wide with panic. "Oh Isaiah," I say and start to cry. I bury my face in my hands as I cry.

"Shh," he whispers. He unbuckles my seatbelt and pulls me into his lap. "You're okay. The baby is okay. I'm okay. There is no need to cry." He kisses my temple. "Calm down, it's all okay. Whatever bad dream it was, it was just a dream nothing more." I nod and wipe my eyes. He rubs my back and kisses me again. "Wanna tell me about your dream? It might make you feel better."

I shake my head no, "It's too painful to tell." He nods and I climb back into the passenger seat.

Isaiah drives for another few hours when we both decide we need to rest for a little while. I pay for the room and Isaiah grabs our stuff. Once in the room Isaiah orders a pizza for us to eat. I shower while we wait for it to get here.

I let the water run down my body. My hand is doing better although it still hurts to use it. I have to scrub my hair with one hand. While I'm standing in the shower I run a hand over my belly. It's hard to believe that me and Isaiah wanting to run off and be happy together led to me getting knocked up. I can't believe it. I'm eight weeks pregnant with Isaiah's baby. Isaiah is my baby's father. "Oh my gosh," I say to myself. "Oh my gosh," I say louder. I turn the water off and get out of the shower.

"What are you saying 'oh my gosh' for?" Isaiah asks me when I open the bathroom door.

"You and me, this," I say waving my hand in a circle around us.

"Yeah, what about it?"

"I just had a huge realization."

"And…? What is it?"

"I got pregnant eight weeks ago. Which means I got pregnant before we left. Which also means I got pregnant that night you came back to Cliff Point," I tell him. He looks as if he's confused. "Eight weeks ago today, you came back to Cliff Point. We slept together then you told me you were falling for me. Eight weeks ago today I conceived this child. I am pregnant with your child. Don't you see? We have been sleeping together for a little more than a year. And then when we decide to run away together we find out I'm pregnant."

"What are you saying?" he asks me.

"Isaiah, this was meant to happen for a reason," I tell him. "Me and you and the baby. Us running off together so we could be happy. That's not what we needed to be happy." I grab his hand and place it on my stomach. "This was. Our child being a surprise was created to bring us closer and make us happy. Don't you see that?" I ask him. "Well not exactly like that but you get what I'm saying."

He grins a little. His boyish grin that reminds me of who he really is and not who he's become. It reminds me of when we first met two years ago. It wasn't until a year ago that we started sleeping together. But when we first met he was so gentle and kind to me. And he grinned like he is now all the time.

"So maybe running away to be happy wasn't what we were supposed to do," he says. "But staying where we were and being there for each other with this little one was all we needed to be happy."

"Exactly," I smile softly up at him. He snakes his arms around me and picks me up.

"Then what do you say we head back home? Find a place and be happy?" he asks me. His grin escalating and reaching his eyes. Alight with joy and love.

"It's a four day trip back home," I say. "If you are up for the journey I am."

He smiles at me then kisses my lips. "With you? Always," he smiles.

He sets me down and wraps my hand. I put on some clothes to sleep in and sit on the bed and start counting what money is left out of the $530,000. I also count cigarettes by the packs and if we need to wash clothes or not. We have $412,000 left; our clothes definantly need to be washed; and there are eight packs of cigarettes left. I've cut back on smoking. I'm trying to quit because of the baby. Isaiah has cut back too but it's going to be harder for him to quit because he has been smoking longer than I have. I can start washing our clothes tonight at the hotel. Get some of them washed and then finish the rest later.

I put the money away and take some of the clothes to the laundry room in the hotel. I get strange looks from the staff considering what I'm wearing. I'm clothed but in a tank top and shorts. I have on a bathrobe so I don't know why they are looking at me weird. I shrug it off and put mine and Isaiah's clothes in the wash. The lady watching over the machines tells me she'll call me when they are finished. She seems sweet so I stay and talk with her for a few minutes.

"How long ya stayin' fer?" she asks me. She's an elderly lady. Dark complexion and brown eyes.

"A day or two," I reply. "Me and my boyfriend are just passing through."

"Ah, headed anywhere in particular?" she asks me.

"Back home," I tell her.

"Lemme' guess," she says. I nod and she continues. "You've run from ya past. Many times, the bof of ya. And this time ya run inta some trouble. Good and bad," she winks at me then continues. "Ya ran to be happy then ya realized that it was no use to keep a runnin' so yous headin' back home."

"Wow, that is spot on," I say quietly. "How did you know that?" I ask her. *Seems weird, if you ask me.* My internal battle has a scared look on her face.

"I've seen many a young couple walk in here the same way you two did," she says. "Worn out and sloppy, forgive me if I insulted ya, and the amount of clothes you put in the wash."

"Oh," I reply and look at my feet. "How did you know me and him were in good and bad trouble?" I ask.

"Oh honey, if yous runnin' from the past there is always bad trouble," she responds. "And I knows the good trouble because yous glowin' chil'," she says. "I'm gonna say eight weeks along? Yeah, happened before ya left too. And ya didn't find out until you left."

How does she do that? "That's exactly right," I say in shock. She grins and grabs my hands. "How did you know all that?"

"Imma great grandma, a grandma, a momma, an auntie, a wife, a sister, and a friend; I always know. And if you two go back home, just know it'll get worse 'fore it gets any better," she tells me. "But ya got the good Lord on ya side. He'll keep ya safe," she adds.

"Thank you," I nod. She nods her head and reminds me that she'll call me when our clothes are finished. I walk back to mine and Isaiah's room and open the door.

"Hey, I thought you'd come right back," he says as he walks towards me. "I thought I was gonna have to come looking for you."

"Sorry, I was talking with this very sweet lady," I tell him. I go sit on the bed and scratch my head.

"What's wrong?" he asks me.

"She said if we go back home it'll get worse before it gets better," I tell him. "She knew everything we are going through. And she said we are making the right decision to go back home."

"Well we will find out when we get back home. Everything will be okay," he reminds me.

"She's gonna call when our clothes are finished," I add. Isaiah nods.

"Why don't you go to sleep, I'll go get our clothes when she calls," he says.

"Okay," I reply. I crawl under the covers and Isaiah kneels beside the bed. He moves the sheets away from my stomach and I grin at him. "What are you doing?"

"I'm gonna talk to the baby," he replies with a small smile. I giggle a little and run my hand over the top of his head. He kisses the center of my belly and I smile.

Isaiah talks to the baby in a soft voice. One I've only heard him use once before. I close my eyes and start to drift off to sleep as Isaiah speaks. A few minutes later I feel the sheets being pulled over me and Isaiah kisses my forehead. I smile and feel the bed dip beside me.

As my slumber pulls me under Isaiah lays his head on my stomach and splays a hand across it. His thumb rubs back and forth in a slow, soft motion. Maybe I was wrong about him. Maybe this is what he always wanted. Someone to love him and give him something that loves him the way he wants to be loved. I love him more than he will ever know and I'm sure our child will love him as much as I do. Isaiah is my everything and I am his. Nothing could ever separate us. Not Snake and Wolf and whatever they have planned for the two of us. Not any distance in the world could separate us. We are one with each other. As I cling to this last thought I drift off into a complete dreamless sleep.

Chapter 11

I wake up to the hotel room door opening and closing. Isaiah comes into view with a basket full of our clothes. She washed and dried them, even folded them for us. I wish more people were like her. Understood kids like me and Isaiah. That would be a perfect world for us to grow up in. No more having to be mean and harsh to others so we get noticed. That's all we've known because society doesn't accept kids like us. We are out casts because we are different and society shouldn't put us down or shun us because we are different. Being different is a good thing.

I watch Isaiah put our clothes back in our bags. He grins when he glances at me. "You should be asleep."

"Come to bed and maybe I'll go back to sleep," I reply with a smile of my own. He shakes his head and holds up a finger letting me know it'll be a minute. I giggle a little and sigh. I wonder who our baby will act like. Me or Isaiah.

Isaiah finishes what he's doing and climbs into bed next to me. He puts his hand on my stomach and rubs softly. "You wanna know something," he says more like a statement than a question.

"What?" I ask him as I run my fingers through his hair.

"When you told me you were pregnant I was horrified," he says. My fingers still in his hair. "I mean we're only eighteen years old and we're going to be parents. But when I thought about it I realized that all I ever wanted was someone to love me the way I needed to be loved when I was growing up. The way I have always wanted to be loved. And you have given me that," he explains. "And more. So much more."

"I thought you would be mad at me and leave," I tell him, my voice trailing off.

"I could never leave you. I've told you this," he replies. It stays silent for a while. Isaiah kisses my stomach every now and then and speaks softly to the baby. Even though I doubt the baby can hear him. He doesn't seem to mind anything that's happening to either of us. All I know is he is happy and I'm happy and that's all I could wish for.

I run my fingers through his hair and he sighs. I look at my phone. I have a voicemail from someone. I open it and listen to it. *"We're coming for Isaiah at noon. No amount of running will save you two,"* Snake's voice hisses over the speaker. I shriek and drop my phone.

"Ouh fuck that hurt," Isaiah says as he rubs his head. "What was that for?" He growls as he sits up.

"The voicemail...Snake...and...and," is all I'm able to say. I'm more afraid now than I ever have been before. For my life. Isaiah's life. And not just us but for our baby's life as well.

I watch Isaiah pick up the phone and listen to the voicemail. His expression grows hard and mean.

He's angry. Really angry. I've never seen him this angry before.

He puts my phone down and warps his arms around me. "Nobody will get you or me or our little one," he tells me. "Just go to sleep. We'll leave at sun up," he adds. I nod and drift back off to sleep.

I don't sleep for long before a nightmare wakes me. Isaiah is there to comfort me and sooth me back to sleep but it doesn't work. Every time I close my eyes all I see is blood. So much blood and it's all Isaiah's. It disturbs me and makes me cling to Isaiah like he's my lifeline. All I care about is him and our baby. When I'm finally able to sleep it's only for an hour.

Isaiah gets me to eat something but I can't eat without thinking about my dream. He keeps reiterating that it's not just me anymore so I'll eat. I eat a little but not enough to satisfy me or the baby.

Day seven on the road is hell. I drift off to sleep for twenty minutes at a time. Isaiah has to stop two or three times for me to get sick and then we head on our way again. I don't know how much more I can take of this. I know we are going back home but we will only be at peace for a short time before Snake realizes we're back.

And when we get home where will we stay? Isaiah slept in his car all the time and that leaves Snake's or Carla's. Snake's place is definantly out because he's looking for Isaiah and myself. That only leaves Carla's. I don't want to go back to her place because then I'll have to explain the whole thing to her and then she'll lecture me about it and throw Isaiah out then Snake will find him for sure.

I can't lose Isaiah. And when Carla finds out I'm pregnant she'll put the baby up for adoption after I have it. I can't lose the baby either. Both of them are a part of me. A part of me I cannot bare to lose.

I guess we'll figure out where to stay later. Hopefully a place on our own but that's doubtful. It was easy in Summersville because nobody there knew us like they do back home. Everyone back home knows us and would easily deny us a place to rent just because of our reputation from Cliff Point.

Isaiah stops the car and gets out. I wonder what for? I've been out of it all day so I haven't been paying attention. I look around and see we're at a gas station. I watch Isaiah walk inside and pay for the gas then walk back out. He sits sideways in the driver's seat while the gas pumps. "Isaiah," I say tiredly. "What time is it?"

"Almost seven," he replies. "We'll stop for something to eat and a place to sleep in a few minutes. The tank was almost empty."

"Okay," I reply. "We're hungry."

He grins and chuckles. He looks over his shoulder at me, "I bet you two are. You hardly ate breakfast and skipped lunch."

"I didn't mean to, I was horrified and I don't eat when I'm horrified," I snap at him.

"I know, it's okay calm down," he says. He gets out of the car and finishes pumping gas in my car. He closes the door behind him then drives off. "Alright, where do you want to eat?" he asks me.

"I don't care," I snap. "Just anywhere will be fine."

"Okay, okay," he replies. He pulls into a drive through, unusual because we always go inside to eat, and orders food for the two of us. He pays and gets our food and drives to a motel. I go pay for the room and Isaiah gets our stuff. He intertwines our fingers as we walk. I smile a little. He's always trying his hardest. He looks down at me and grins.

When we find our room I sit on the bed and start to eat. Isaiah watches me as I eat. He's concerned about my well-being because of what happened yesterday. I understand he's worried about me. He doesn't need to be, I can look after myself. But he loves me and wants to care for me. "I'm gonna shower," I tell him when I finish eating. He nods and I slip into the bathroom.

I look down at my belly and see a tiny bump forming. This is all too real. I can't believe this is happening to me. I never wanted kids because I'm afraid I'll turn out like Carla. Marry a dead beat guy who is a dead beat dad who leaves his family behind. Then make my kid go crazy and turn them into a junky like me. But yet here I am. In a hotel room in Tennessee with a baby in my belly. Who would have thought, Sheryl, a girl with a badass nickname, pregnant with a kid at eighteen? I never imagined it and I bet nobody at Cliff Point would have imagined it either.

I know I didn't! Oh shut it, I don't need you right now.

I step out of the shower and wrap a towel around my body. I walk out of the bathroom and start putting on my sleep clothes when Isaiah stops me. "Claw, turn to the side and stand up straight." I do as he says and he walks closer to me. "Is someone starting to show?" he asks. I nod and bite my lower lip.

"Stop biting your lip, this is great," he says as he pulls on my chin making me release my lower lip. "Why do you look so worried?"

"Because I'm gonna start getting fatter and I don't want you to turn away from me because of it," I tell him.

"Hey, I don't give a shit if you gain four hundred pounds. I will still love you," he replies. "This is our baby we are talking about. It's growing and this shows that everything is okay. I'm not gonna turn away from you because your belly is growing to accommodate what's inside it."

"Really?"

"Yes, really," he whispers and kisses me gently. I smile through our kiss. Isaiah smiles too and lifts me up off the floor. He lays me on the bed and kisses all over me. "How are we gonna keep this a secret when we get back home?" he asks me.

"Well until I grow a huge belly it'll be easy. But eventually people will find out," I tell him. He nods. "We'll figure it out later. There is a lot to figure out later but we'll get it done, don't worry."

"Okay," he replies.

Isaiah lays his head on my belly and rubs it gently like he always does. Being away from Cliff Point for a while has made us realize we no longer need to be angry at the world. We were just damaged people trying to find ourselves. All we ever need is acceptance. And we found it in each other. That's all we needed. When we return to Cliff Point nothing will be the same. There will be a new leader and possibly new people there as well. But I don't think we will go to Cliff Point unless we need to just go for old times' sake.

"What will we name our baby?" Isaiah asks me, breaking the silence.

"I'm not sure," I reply. "I guess we'll find out later," I tell him. "But I do need to see a doctor soon. You know to see how everything is going with the baby."

Isaiah nods, "okay. Well find one tomorrow to visit and check on everything."

"Sounds like a plan."

Me and Isaiah sit in silence for a while. Him just rubbing my belly and me running my fingers through his thick, black hair. Me and Isaiah don't need words to express what we feel or think all the time. Sometimes silence is just enough to say what needs saying. Silence is always telling. It can be either good or bad. In most instances its bad but in our case it's almost always good.

Isaiah grabs my phone and starts going through it. I have nothing to hide so I don't bother to take it from him.

"There is a new message from Snake," he tells me.

"Hmm," I respond. "What else is new? There's always a message from snake on my phone."

"'I am the new leader of Cliff Point as of today. When you two decide to return I'll be waiting with the guys,' is all it says," Isaiah tells me.

"Well, I figured as much that he would become leader," I say. "He was highest ranking after me. After him is Wolf," I explain.

"What about me?" he asks out of curiosity.

"Well if you had been around more, then you would have been after me, then Snake, then Wolf," I explain. "But then again you were never around so you got booted out of line on that front I'm afraid."

"Oh, but then we both ran away together so Snake would have been leader anyway," he responds.

"Exactly."

It gets quiet again and my eyes close. I feel Isaiah press his lips to my belly. "Good night little one," he whispers. He leans up and kisses me softly on the nose. "Goodnight Sheryl," he whispers. He hasn't called me that in a while. Maybe it's because we've been away from Cliff Point for so long that I no longer need the nickname.

Or maybe it's because he loves you enough to no longer call you by your nickname. Didn't think of that did you? I roll my eyes at her. But then again she could be right.

"Goodnight Isaiah," I whisper. I curl up on my side and Isaiah pulls me into him. The warmth of his body envelopes me and I breathe out a sigh of contentment. "I love you."

"I love the both of you," he replies and kisses my cheek. He wraps his arms around my middle and pats my belly. I smile softly and drift off to sleep.

Chapter 12

Day eight on the road. Or day one of heading home. Isaiah woke up just before sunrise and woke me up not long after. We've been driving for about three hours to kill time until a doctor's office is open. It's taken us longer to get back to Louisville because we have to stop so much. Stopping for breakfast, gas, lunch, gas again, then dinner and a place to sleep at night. And now add a visit to a doctor for me, it's gonna take a while.

My hand has healed considerably well since I pretty much broke it punching the hotel shower wall a few days ago. *I'll admit that was my fault for the hand.* I roll my eyes at her, of course it was.

I can squeeze my hand and make a fist without much pain so that's a good sign. Isaiah has been remotely silent in the past three hours. He's probably thinking of where we will stay once we get back to Louisville. When we first got on the road this morning we had an argument over where to stay. Since then he's been silent. Looking at me every now and then. I wonder what he's thinking about.

"There's a hospital at the next exit," he starts. "We'll stop there." Very short, unusual for him. Unless he's angry or overthinking something.

I nod, "Okay." He doesn't respond he just glares at me. He hates when I just say 'okay'. It stays silent for a few more minutes. "Is something wrong?" I ask breaking the silence.

"Nothing," he replies. Short and clipped.

He's angry, scared. All things he can't express. You of all people should know this!

"Dammit Isaiah, would you tell me what's wrong?"

"I'm just trying to figure this shit out, okay Sheryl?" he retorts. "I have no idea where we are gonna stay once we get back to Louisville. I don't know how long we will be there before we get seen and Snake finds us. I'm just trying to figure this shit out." He smacks the steering wheel with the palm of his hand. He's angry and upset and scared all at once and he doesn't know how to handle his emotions.

I grab his hand and kiss his palm. I place his hand on my stomach, "Isaiah everything will be okay. We will figure it out together." He shakes his head like it won't and never will be. "Isaiah stop the car." He looks at me funny.

"Why the fuck for?" he snaps.

"Just stop the damn car," I snap at him. He does as I say and pulls over and turns my car off. I turn sideways in my seat and look at him. "Would you please for the love of God just tell me what you're feeling?"

He stays silent for a while. He's thinking of how to form his sentences to explain something he's never had to explain. His emotions. Tons of emotions cross his face and he tries to settle for one but can't. "Isaiah tell me, don't over think it. Just say it."

He breathes in deep and hangs his head. "Sheryl, I'm scared. I'm angry and upset and worried. All these emotions I'm having I've never had before and it scares me. I don't know how to express them. I've never had to before," he explains. "All this shit is confusing."

I lean forward and place my hands on either side of his face and lift his head to look at me. Watery eyes meet mine. "Isaiah everything will be alright," I whisper to him. I can't believe I'm about to say this but here goes, "how about this, I'll call Carla when we get close to Louisville. I'll call her and see if we can stay there. If she says yes then when we get there I will explain the situation to her, alright?"

Well it's about time you cried mom. I slap my internal battle and she just sits there and grins. I fucking hate when she's right all the time.

"What if she says no?" he asks me. His face marked with tension and fear.

"If she says no then we drive there anyway and explain it," I tell him. "Either way Carla is our only option of living anywhere right now."

"Okay, call Carla after we leave the hospital," he sighs.

I nod. "You okay now?"

"Yeah, I'm okay," he whispers. Although his body language and facial expression says he's not okay. He's anything but.

"Good," I say and kiss him. He smiles a small smile when I pull away and then he starts my car and drives down the road.

A little while later he pulls off the interstate and drives to the nearby hospital. He parks the car and we walk inside. An orderly directs us where to go and soon we are sitting in an OBGYN's waiting room.

"Sheryl!" I hear my name called. Me and Isaiah get up and follow a nurse to a room. The nurse weighs me and then takes me to another room. She asks me a series of questions that seem to go on forever.

Do I smoke? Do I drink? How old am I? Is Isaiah the father? Was I rapped? Do I want the baby? All the ongoing stupid questions. "The doctor will be in with you in a moment," she says and walks out.

"How many damn questions was she going to ask before she left?" Isaiah asks me. He runs a hand through his hair and sighs. His hair has gotten considerably longer in the last week. I don't like it. I wonder if he'd let me cut it?

Not with scissors that close to his head with your hormones mixed with your bad temper! I roll my eyes. It's not that bad.

"Don't know, but gah it makes me wanna smoke," I say. Although I'm quitting, I still smoke at least three to four cigarettes a day. It's less than the one and a half packs a day I used to smoke.

"You're trying to quit remember?"

"Yeah, yeah," I reply.

"And I'm not gonna give you one either. I'm tryin' to quit myself, for your's and the baby's sake," he explains. It warms my heart to hear he's trying to quit for the baby.

"Isaiah, I wanna cut your hair," I tell him. He looks at me with a shocked expression and I laugh.

"Whatever possessed you to ask that question?" he asks me just as shocked as his facial expression.

"It's getting long and I don't like it," I reply. "I've cut my own hair before."

He sighs and runs a hand through his hair, "Well I guess if my girlfriend doesn't like it, I'll cut it. But I will cut it. I always cut my hair," he tells me. Firm in his decision.

"Alrighty," I grin and nod.

We stay silent until the door opens again. "Hello, I'm Dr. Chin," I male doctor says as he shakes mine and Isaiah's hands. "The nurse has already asked these questions but I have to ask them, too," he explains and asks the same stupid questions I answered earlier. "Alright, now I understand you two are traveling?" he questions.

"Yes," I say. "Headed back home."

"Alright, and I'm sure once you get home you will find a permanent doctor to see about your pregnancy?"

"Yes," I say and Isaiah nods.

"Alright then, let's take a look at your baby," he says. I lift my shirt and he squirts cool gel on my stomach. He rolls a machine around and I can see a computer screen. He rolls a wand around my belly. The whole time intently starring at the screen. I start to hear what sounds like a tiny heartbeat. "That's the baby's heartbeat," he tells us. "And there," he pauses the screen. "Is your baby. Everything looks normal. I'm sure you have vitamins to take to keep the two of you healthy but in case you are running out or don't, here is some to take. I suggest getting more when you two get home," he explains.

Me and Isaiah nod. Dr. Chin hands me paper towel and I wipe my stomach off. "See a doctor as soon as you get home. That's all, you are free to go," he tells us.

Isaiah helps me off the table and we leave.

Everyone here looks at us funny. It puts me on edge and I don't like it. Isaiah can feel that I'm uneasy and puts an arm around me. Everyone probably looks at us like we're gonna rob them. My clothes being tighter than normal because I'm pregnant. Isaiah looks angry all the time, but it's just his everyday facial expression.

Unless he's looking only at you! I grin shyly at her, she's right about that.

But I'm pretty sure we would get weird looks anyway, even if we weren't from where we are from. Isaiah is a whole foot taller than me with tattoos all over his body. We look like an odd couple as it is.

"Fuckin' pricks," he mumbles as we exit the building.

"Isaiah," I scold him. He gives me his I-really-don't-care-scold-me-all-you-want look and I huff and cross my arms over my chest. "People don't understand us. They never have and they probably never will."

"They never have and they never will," he retorts, relaying my words making them true. "It'll be the same our whole lives. Always gettin' odd looks 'cause of my tats and 'cause we're young parents. Our child will live with that hanging over his or her shoulders. Don't you get it Sheryl?"

"Isaiah, is that what's worrying you?" I ask him. He sighs and looks at the ground and nods his head slightly. "Isaiah, who gives a shit what people think of us? And we will teach our child to do the same, shrug off what people think and how they look at us. Because it doesn't matter what those people think. It only matters of what we think of ourselves. Don't you see Isaiah? Who cares what they think about us, or our baby. Everything is going to be fine, okay?"

"Okay," he whispers. I reach up and kiss him. I hear a car honk at us, Isaiah looks at them and flips them off then grabs my hand and we find my car.

We get to my car and Isaiah gets back on the interstate. "Isaiah, we're hungry," I yawn. "And tired."

He laughs a little. "I'll stop and get us some food then you can sleep," he tells me. I nod and yawn again. "I hope McDonalds is okay, cause that is our only option right now," he explains.

"That's fine," I tell him. I see him nod and he stops and gets us something to eat. "Thanks," I say when he hands me mine.

"No problem, just eat since you didn't eat a lot at breakfast," he tells me. "You can't just keep skipping meals anymore," he adds.

"I know," I sigh. "I'm just worried about the whole going back home situation."

Isaiah reaches across and puts his hand on my belly. "I will not let anything or anyone hurt you or our baby," he tells me. His tone firm and serious. "I mean that Sheryl."

I nod and finish eating. I fall asleep soon after.

"Sheryl wake up," I hear Isaiah whisper. He nudges me gently.

"Isaiah where are we?" I ask sleepily and rub my eyes.

"We're back in Kentucky, in Summersville," he explains. "Come on, I'll carry you," he says and picks me up.

"No, I can walk," I tell him. He steps back and I get out of the car. I notice he has food in his hand. When did he stop again? Oh well I'm just glad he bought more for us to eat. I grab our stuff and we pay for a hotel room for the night.

"I'm gonna shower," I tell Isaiah when we get in the room.

"Okay, don't take too long. You need to eat while it's still warm," he tells me.

"Yeah, yeah," I say and close the bathroom door behind me. I step in the shower and just stand under the running water. I have to call Carla even though I don't want to. Hopefully she'll let me back in the house and let me explain the situation. Even if she says no, she has to hear what I have to say.

Of course she'll let you come back home! She's been begging you to come back home for weeks.

The whole running thing didn't work out as planned. Even if me and Isaiah were to run all the way to California, Snake would still find us. But running has made us realize we don't need to run to be happy. All the sneaking around we did wasn't necessary but we did it anyway. We found ourselves in the process of all this. I jump when I hear a knock at the door.

"Sheryl, get out of the shower so you can eat," I hear Isaiah shout. "Your food's getting' cold out here."

"Alright, damn give me a minute," I snap back. I turn the shower off and wrap a towel around my body. I walk out of the bathroom and over to my food and eat a bite. "There, happy?" I spit at him.

"I would be if you would eat the whole thing," he retorts. "And if you would lose the attitude," he adds.

I growl at him and sit on the other bed and eat. Isaiah stares at me the whole time. "I'm eating, stop fucking staring at me," I say harshly. He turns his head away and looks at the wall. I look down and realize I'm only in a towel. That's probably why he's staring at me. I glance at him and he's staring at me again. I shake my head at him. "You're only staring at me because I'm in a towel."

"Maybe," he says slowly. I look at him, his eyes are burning grey. His whole body seems to radiate what he wants.

I get up and throw my trash in the garbage. I can feel Isaiah watching me the whole time. I stand in front of the mirror above the sink and brush my teeth. I jump when Isaiah's hands rest on my hips. "Shh, it's just me," he whispers. He can walk so lightly, but other times he walks so hard. "You being angry has turned me on." I can hear the smirk in his voice.

"Oh has it?" I question.

"Yes," he kisses my neck, "it has."

"What are you gonna do about it?" I ask and cock my hip to the side. Bumping into him on purpose.

"Many, many things," he growls low in his throat. A sound that drives me nuts. "First I'm gonna do this," he says and turns me around. He lifts me up on the counter and pushes my legs apart. "Wrap your legs around me," he demands. I do as he says and he starts kissing my neck. He picks me up off the counter and carries me to the bed. "I don't think you need this anymore," he says and toss's my towel across the room. He trails kisses down my body then back up. Stopping momentarily to glance up at me as he kisses my stomach.

He grins as he kisses my stomach. He looks back up at me again and his eyes go soft momentarily. He looks breathtaking.

I pull Isaiah's shirt off and trace the tattoo along his side. The dragon that runs up most of his back. The tail runs down his side. I moan as he kisses my neck just below my ear. I lift my hips off the bed and feel him. "Take me," I moan.

"In due time babe," he smirks. I huff and moan at the same time.

Fifteen minutes later the two of us are laying breathless on the bed. I'm curled up next to Isaiah's side. His arms wrapped around me, I feel safe. I've always felt safe with Isaiah but I feel safest when I'm in his arms.

He runs his hands up and down my back gently. My phone rings breaking the silence between us. "Who is it?" Isaiah asks me.

"Fuck, its Carla," I say. I sit up and answer the phone. "Hello?"

"Sheryl, I figured you wouldn't answer," she says sadly.

"Actually, I needed to talk to you," I tell her. I feel Isaiah's hand on my back.

"What about?" she asks.

"I wanna come home," I tell her. "But I have something to explain first."

Don't tell her you're pregnant yet!

"Alright, what is it?" she asks me. She sounds excited, oh shit.

I give her the short version. "It's not just me, Isaiah is with me and we both need a place to stay. Snake and everyone from Cliff Point is looking for us," I explain.

"There is something else here that you're not telling me," she states.

And for the first time in six years, "mom, I'll tell you when we get there. Just can we stay or not?"

"Sheryl you called me mom," she gushes. "Yes you can stay here."

Awe! My internal battle gushes. *You called her mom!*

"Thanks mom," I smile. I hang up the phone and look at Isaiah. "We have a place to stay. The only thing she doesn't know is that I'm pregnant," I explain to him. "Yet."

"You called her mom," he says. He grins at me and starts making fun of me.

"I know I did," I reply and lay back down, stopping his attempts to say anything. "It was the only way for her to stop talking and agree to let us stay."

"I'm glad we have a place to stay now," he says and kisses the top of my head. "Let's go to sleep. We've got a three hour drive tomorrow back to Carla's."

"I know, and a long conversation once we get there," I say.

"Yup, one I don't really want to have with Carla but she needs to know," he tells me.

"Good night Isaiah," I yawn. "I love you."

"Good night Sheryl, I love you too," he replies. And with that I drift.

Chapter 13

I texted Carla before we left saying that we are three hours away from her house. I could hear the smile in her voice last night when I said I wanted to come home. And by wanted I mean: I have no choice so could you please let us stay cause me and my boyfriend, the father to my child, are being chased. Yeah, she so would have bought that one.

I'm sure if you told her she probably would just because you called her mom last night.

Anyway, Isaiah put our stuff in my car after he woke up. He doesn't sleep much at night because of what's going on. I watch as he walks around. Shirtless as always, his tattoo twists and moves with his movements and looks as if it could fly off his back. The serpent on his left arm, if he flexes just right, looks as if it could strike at someone. Then there's the tattoo on his right arm. I'm not sure what it is but it appears to be something of a lion of sorts. Maybe a cheetah I'm not sure.

"Whatcha you looking at," he grins at me. He seems in an exceptionally good mood this morning.

"Your tattoos," I reply with a smile of my own. He laughs. "I know what the one on your back and left arm is but I don't know what the one on your right arm is."

"It's a cheetah," he replies. He looks away quickly.

"Oh," I say.

He nods his head then we head out on the road. Halting all talk of his tattoos completely.

He stops to get us breakfast and then stops to get gas. He holds my hand all the way down the road. "I have a story to tell you," he says breaking the silence.

"Is it good or bad?"

"Depends on how you wanna see it," he tells me. "It's good I guess."

"Okay, onward with the story," I tell him. I smile at him and he smiles a shy smile.

"My tattoos, they mean something," he says. "Each one has a different meaning behind it. But it goes further than just the ink. It's the size that helps account for the story. I got the dragon first, the serpent next, and the cheetah last. The dragon, it's the largest because it proves how big I want to be. Not just what I'm known for. Dragons are fierce and fight for their territory. I got it when I was sixteen. Up until then I thought tattoos were stupid. Then I wanted them to mean something.

"Anyway, I was always in fights, protecting what's mine. I had this guy, who was always sleeping with my mom whom I thought would be my new dad, I still talk with him, tell me that I had a right to protect what's mine and I had a spit fire mouth when it came to telling someone off. Hence why I have a dragon breathing fire.

"The serpent on my left arm, I got it when I was seventeen. The reason it looks coiled and ready to strike is because I can strike on someone at any moment. Just like the snake can. Believe it or not my mother talked me into getting it. She saw the way I could react at the drop of a hat and told me I am the serpent in everyone's life. This was before she went completely bat shit crazy and became a whore to support us. Hence the reason I slept in my car all the time. I couldn't stand all the guys coming in my home just to have one night stands with her. Some of the guys beat her and even me, if they were angry enough.

"Anyway after I got it, it seemed a stupid tattoo because my mother talked me into getting it. But looking at it now, now it just reminds me of what I got away from. I couldn't live with her after she became what she became. I would strike out at the men she would bring home. That was a month after I got the tattoo." He falls silent.

"Isaiah, you got away from her," I remind him. "And you've made out just fine. Well until now."

"Yeah, I know I did," he replies. "And I'm glad I did. I probably wouldn't be here with you if I hadn't gotten out. I'd probably be in juvie hall."

"What's the cheetah mean?" I ask. It's been bothering me since he turned away when I asked him what it was.

"That one, I got it six months ago," he smiles.

"Why are you smiling?"

It's for you! He got it for you! My inner battle screams with joy and jumps up and down. I'm glad I'm not as hyper as she is.

"It's when I started following you around," he explains. "Every time I approached you, you ran because you had to go. Cheetahs run fast and by golly you ran fast. I would blink and you'd be gone. But you also have a cheetahs grace and ease. You get angry in a split second and could devour someone quickly. I had it inked in laying down because that's when you're at your most calm, such as the cheetah. I got it when I started falling for you," he turns his head to look at me then looks back at the road.

"Isaiah," I whisper. "What if we hadn't worked out?"

"Then I would still have it. A crash and burn memory that would be with me forever. Much like the serpent," he explains. "And after the baby is born I'm gonna get one for the baby. Haven't figured out what it's gonna be but it'll be an animal of some sort."

"Isaiah, you don't have to do that," I tell him.

Would you shut up and listen to the boy! I shoot her a look and she crosses her arms and glares at me.

"I do, for me," he explains. "That child is part of me. Therefore it has earned a place on my skin. It's another story to tell. And a story I will never forget."

"Isaiah," I say as I start to cry. Damn these pregnancy hormones! I'm always angry or crying. The angry part worse than before but the crying, I never cried this much.

"I mean that Sheryl," he whispers and puts his hand on my stomach. I look down at my stomach. It's getting bigger every day; soon it will be hard to hide it. I've got to hide it for as long as I can. Even if it means wearing Isaiah's clothes. Which I have no problem with; they smell of him and make me feel safe.

He keeps his hand where it is the rest of the trip to Carla's house. I text her saying we're getting close. If she was on the phone talking to me, she would be all gushy about me coming home.

"Carla is okay with this right?" Isaiah asks me. He feels uneasy about it.

"Yes, over joyed actually," I say. "I haven't been home for three months."

"When are we gonna break the news about tiny tot there?" he asks me. He grins as he says it. Which in turn makes me grin.

"Good question," I say. "She'll probably see it. My clothes hug my stomach tighter than they did before. Either she'll think I'm just getting fat or I'm pregnant. Either way she'll ask about it. Then we'll sit her down and tell her."

"I don't wanna break the news to her," he says and runs a hand over the top of his head. "What if she kicks me out? Or both of us? Then has you put the baby up for adoption after it's born?" Wow, he really is worried about all this. More so than I am.

He's worried about the same things you are. His fear is worse than yours because he can't risk losing you.

"Isaiah, I've thought about it, too. She can do what she wants, but I will not give up this baby," I explain to him. "Where the baby goes I go. There is no taking it from me."

"You're set in stone with this aren't ya?" he asks me.

"Yes, very much so. And I would hope you are, too," I snap at him. "Cause if not then we have a serious problem."

"I go where ever our child goes," he tells me. "I will fight to the ends of the earth to protect our child and keep it with us."

For the first time in Isaiah's life he has something to call his own. Besides me. I never thought he would be this protective over an accident. And if he says he's in this for the long haul then he really is. He never turns his back on his word. Ever.

The whole time Isaiah and I have been together I've seen a change in him. He's not as cold as he used to be. Or angry. If anything he's learning to be an adult. Both of us are actually. Eighteen year olds becoming parents. It's enough to freak anyone out. It makes parents wonder what they did wrong but our parents wouldn't care. Well, Carla might but his mother could care less.

I watch as Isaiah stares at the road ahead of us. Leading us to Carla's. Hopefully we won't get seen by anyone. Cause if Jack sees us, he's bound to snitch to Snake and Wolf that we're back and staying at Carla's.

"We're here," Isaiah tells me. His tone nervous.

I just nod. "Park over there," I tell him and point to the empty spot next to the garage. It's hidden in the trees so nobody can see my car. "You ready for this?"

"As I'll ever be, but if means keeping you two safe then yes I am," he replies. I nod and we get out of my car.

Carla meets us at the front door, "Oh Sheryl thank goodness you're home," she gushes and envelopes me in a hug. She's crying, you've got to be kidding me.

And in order for us to stay here I have to keep calling her mom. "Mom, this is Isaiah," I tell her. She hugs him, too for some strange reason. "We need to get inside mom. So we can explain everything," I tell her.

"Of course," she says and ushers us in the house. I see the house looks cleaner. "I left your room the way you did when you left," she tells me. I nod. "You two want anything?" She eyes Isaiah nervously. She probably thinks he's gonna rob her or something. Pull out a shank and kill her, I don't know. Carla has an odd take on people she's never met before.

"I'm okay," Isaiah says.

"Me too," I tell her. I have my denim jacket on, easy way to hide my growing stomach. "We need to explain the situation at hand."

"Alright we can talk in the living room," she says. We walk in the living room and Isaiah and I sit on the couch. I pull my jacket over my stomach to hide it until I tell her. "I'm guessing this is the long version?" she asks. Isaiah nods.

"Me and Isaiah were sneaking around to see each other. Snake and Wolf don't like Isaiah at all. So we left. Ran off together so we could be happy. Snake wants to find us and hurt, if not kill, Isaiah," I explain.

Carla nods. "If you wanted to be happy, why did you run?" she asks us. "Running shouldn't constitute happiness. You two should be happy regardless of the situation at hand."

"All we did was sneak around so no one knew we were together," Isaiah tells her with an edge to his voice. "We were happy, we just wanted to be happy away from the danger."

"Isaiah she's right," I tell him. "But we have two problems. One Snake doesn't realize that Isaiah won't hurt me and never will." I pause.

"Okay, what is the second problem?" she asks breaking the silence.

Here it goes, "I'm pregnant."

Boom. Pregnancy bomb on the whole thing. Carla's facial expression doesn't change. I take my denim jacket off to show my belly. Then her facial expression changes.

"And Isaiah, he's the um...the father?" she stutters. Her eyes glued to my belly.

"Yes, I am," he replies coldly. He doesn't like her starring. Even though she can stare at me. I'm her daughter after all.

"Sheryl how far along are you?" she asks.

"Almost three and a half months."

"And you two plan on keeping the baby?" We both nod. "And you've seen a doctor hopefully?" We nod again. She sags with relief, slightly. "How are you two gonna go see a doctor and not be seen by Snake?" she asks. Wow the first logical question to ask for our situation at hand.

Would you cool it please?

"That's where we were hoping you could help us," Isaiah says. His voice calming. He doesn't seem as nervous as when we arrived.

"Mom, I know you're a nurse in that department, and you're really good friends with one of the main doctors there. We were hoping you could pull some strings to help us out," I say.

"Sheryl, I don't know," she says. She runs a hand over her face. She leaves her hand over her mouth.

I get up and kneel in front of her. I start to cry. Damn these hormones. "Mom, you have to help us please," I beg her. I take her free hand and place it on my stomach. "Not for just me and Isaiah, but for our baby, too. Your grandchild."

"Don't cry Sheryl," she says and wipes my face off. "Those hormones suck though don't they?" she asks with a smile. I smile and nod my head. "I'll see what I can do," she tells me. "In the meantime, I have plenty of those vitamins you need to keep you and the baby healthy. You two go upstairs and get some sleep. I'll call Dr. Bates in a few minutes."

Chapter 14

"Sheryl wake up," I hear as someone nudges me.

"Let me sleep," I groan and roll over.

"You need to wake up, I have to tell you something," I realize its Carla.

"I'm up," I say and sit up. Isaiah is still asleep.

"I made breakfast, let's talk downstairs," she tells me. I nod and follow her downstairs. We reach the kitchen and I fix myself a plate and sit down to eat. "I called Dr. Bates this morning. I told her the situation at hand and she said she will make trips to the house for your appointments. However, if you two are still hiding from Snake six months from now when you go into labor, I have to take you to the hospital," she explains.

"I figured as much," I reply. I finish eating my food in silence. Carla brings me more. I guess she can tell how hungry I am. "Thanks," I tell her. Even though me and Isaiah stopped for food, we haven't had a good home cooked meal in a while.

"You're welcome," she replies. "I hope you two understand how much of a responsibility a child is. Feeding it, caring for it when it's sick, and all the things that come with having a baby. It gets hard at times; I hope you two know that."

"We do," I reply. "We've talked about it and we know what we are up against with this. We are both willing to try our hardest at this."

"I hope you are," she murmurs. She looks as if she's about to cry.

"Mom, don't cry," I say and hug her. I mean after all she is my mother, even if we don't see eye to eye I still love her.

"I can't believe you're pregnant," she sniffles. She holds me away from her at arm's length. "Did I do anything wrong? What made you this way?" she asks. I sigh, how many times do I have to explain it to her?

"It wasn't you mom," I tell her. "It was dad, when he left and you started working more to support us. You were never there for me. Okay it was partially you. I was alone. I started going to Cliff Point because everyone there had my back. That's when the smoking and drinking started. Then came sleeping with almost every guy there. Until I met Isaiah. Isaiah is the only guy I've slept with in the last year," I explain to her. "I found out I was pregnant after we left. I was two months pregnant then. And now I'm three and a half."

"Sheryl I'm so sorry," she says and pulls me to her. "Dr. Bates will be here in an hour. She's gonna ask the same questions you've heard from other doctors about this. Don't get angry with her. Please," she begs. "I know how your temper is. And I'm betting with the hormones its worse."

"I won't," I tell her. She nods and takes my empty plate from me. I walk upstairs into my room. The bed is empty. Isaiah was still asleep when I went downstairs earlier. I hear a noise from my closet.

"What are you doing?" I ask him.

"Figured I would see what kind of secrets you have hidden in the depths of your closet," Isaiah tells me.

"Oh, like pictures of my dead beat father and of when I was little," I snap at him. "It's all part of my past that I despise."

"What about these?" he asks me and holds up two stuffed unicorns. Slits in their sides where stuffing is falling out of them.

"Don't touch those," I say and snatch them from him. Causing more stuffing to fall to the floor.

"Why not?" he asks me. "There is a story behind them, isn't there?" He looks intrigued, smiling broadly.

"Yes," I say and sit on the bed. "Two years before my father left he gave me these. He told me he would never leave me. When he left I cut them open. I ripped the hearts out just like my father ripped out mine. One is him and the other is my mother. Both of them ripped my heart out. So I did it to the unicorns. It's not normal for a twelve year old to do that, but I did it anyway."

"They may have ripped your heart out but I put it back," he whispers and kisses me. I drop the unicorns to the floor and we fall back on my bed. I wrap my arms around his neck. We stop when there is a knock at my door. "Damn, are we ever gonna get passed kissing?"

"It's probably Dr. Bates, she agreed to come here. Up until the baby is born," I tell him. He nods. "Come in," I say. The door opens and Carla and Dr. Bates walk in my room. Dr. Bates is a tall dark skin woman. Short black hair with brown eyes. She's a beautiful woman.

"Sheryl, Isaiah, this is Dr. Bates," Carla introduces us.

"I have been notified of the situation and I will do all your appointments here up until the baby is born. When you go into labor you will have to go to the hospital," she tells us. Me and Isaiah nod.

Dr. Bates goes into all the same questions I've been asked twice before. I guess the third time's the charm right? Anyway, we stay in my room the whole time. Dr. Bates does an ultrasound and writes stuff down as she goes. Everyone stays silent the entire time. Carla leans against my dresser, Isaiah sits beside me, and I'm laying flat on my bed. When she finishes, Dr. Bates hands me a paper towel to wipe my stomach off with.

"I estimate you are three and a half months pregnant. I've given your mother the vitamins you need to take for you and your baby's health. How many cigarettes do you smoke a day now?" she asks me.

"Three to four," I tell her.

"I'm guessing you're trying to quit?" I nod. "Good, no more drinking either. It's not good for the baby for you to keep smoking and drinking. It can cause birth defects and the drinking can cause the infant to be born wanting alcohol."

"Oh," I say. I sit up on my bed and Isaiah puts a hand on my belly. I didn't realize it was such a huge risk. I mean I haven't had a drink since I found out I was pregnant, but still.

"Now that you have started showing I suggest wearing bigger clothes. The ones you currently have on will not fit in a few weeks or in a few months. You are at a good weight right now being almost four months pregnant. And I thoroughly suggest eating three whole meals a day every day," she explains. "That wraps up this appointment, I'll be back in four weeks to check up on you and your baby again." And with that she leaves.

I snuggle up to Isaiah and he wraps his arms around me. Carla walks to the foot of the bed and stops. "What are you gonna wear?" she asks me and folds her arms over her chest.

"Isaiah's clothes," I tell her. "He doesn't mind if I do."

"I think it looks damn sexy when you do," he says. "It drives me nuts," he growls. I laugh and kiss him.

"Sheryl, I'll buy you something to wear."

"Mother, no. I'll wear Isaiah's clothes," I protest.

"Fine, wear what you want to wear. In the meantime, I've washed all of your clothes and I'll bring them up here. I'll be back in a few minutes," she says and then she walks out.

When my door closes I throw a leg over Isaiah and sit on top of him. "Carla will catch us," he says as I kiss him.

"I don't care," I moan. "I'm extremely turned on by your statement."

"Oh are you?"

"Uh huh," I moan. He grabs my hips and flips us so I'm beneath him. I hear my door open but don't pay attention to it.

"I understand you two are having a baby, but having sex all the time is not going to be allowed in this house," Carla says.

Isaiah starts kissing my neck. "This is the first time we've even done this since we got here," I tell her.

"Okay, I guess it's too late to tell you to use protection," she says and walks out.

Hehe Carla does have a valid point, my internal battle laughs. I ignore her and focus on Isaiah and the here and now.

"Fuck it," Isaiah says and pulls mine and his pants off. Soon the both of us are in a tangle of sheets and skin.

Isaiah lays beside me in the aftermath and rubs my belly. "That was different," he says.

"Good different or bad different?"

"Good different," he replies.

"Isaiah do you realize what you did?"

"No, what'd I do?" He swallows hard and looks anxiously up at me. Worry and fear etched all over his beautiful face.

"You made love to me," I tell him. I sit up and look at him. He looks confused. "Both of us going slow, taking our time at this and not rushing it like we always do. We made love to each other."

Isaiah just nods. I don't think he likes the idea of making love to each other. I grab his hand and he just looks at me. "Did you not enjoy it?" I ask him quietly.

"I did, it's just...different. I've never done that before and I don't know what it makes me feel," he explains.

Oh Lord, here we go again. You better get him to explain his emotions or something bad will come of this! Which she's right, I need to get him to explain himself. I don't want him running or hiding from this.

"About me or what it makes you feel about all this?" I ask worried he's turning away from me already.

He could never turn away from you! Don't think like that Sheryl! But what if he is? I'm so confused. *Stop getting confused! It's making me confused too!*

"No, Sheryl it's not about you," he says to reassure me. "I think I've reached this whole new level of love that I didn't know was there and I don't know how to express it."

"Isaiah you just did," I tell him. "You making love to me showed that whole new level." He just nods his head. "I'm hungry, so I'm gonna go downstairs and find something to eat. You want anything?" I ask him.

"Nah, I'm good," he smiles a small smile. I smile back, kiss him gently, and walk downstairs.

Don't leave him alone! My internal battle screams at me. I'll only be a few minutes. Not too long, besides what is he gonna do in the span of a few minutes? I just want food.

"You two done up there?" Carla asks me.

"Yes, and I'm hungry," I tell her. "I mean we're hungry."

"There's food in the fridge and in the pantry. Help yourself," she tells me. I see her smile a little. She is excited that she's becoming a grandma.

I sit down in front of her with a bag of chips. She's paying bills like always. "You still pulling double shifts at the hospital?" I ask her.

"No, I got a raise so I don't have to anymore," she tells me. "Plus I'm still working even at home now because you're pregnant."

"Mom, I can take care of myself," I tell her. With a twinge of anger in my voice. I've always taken care of myself.

"I know you can. I was just teasing with you," she grins. "Calm down. Please."

"Don't do that," I say angrily.

"Hey, calm the hormones a little," she tells me. "Dr. Bates talked with me a little before she left. She said despite how much you smoked before you found out you were pregnant didn't harm the baby. So there is a good thing so far."

"And let me guess a bad thing is about to fall isn't it?" I ask.

"Not always, nothing bad to report right now," she says.

Yes there is! I ignore her. Everything is alright right now. *No it's not!* Oh shut it snarky bitch.

"Alrighty then, I'll be upstairs," I tell her. She nods and I walk upstairs. When I reach my room, I find it empty. I search every room upstairs and start to panic. M heat beating a mile a minute. This can't be happening. I don't need anything else to go wrong. I run down the stairs. "Mom!" I yell in a panic.

I told you but you don't listen to me. When do you ever listen to me?

"Sheryl, what is it? Calm down," she tells me.

"It's Isaiah," I tell her. I'm shaking and scared. I don't know where he is. I can't lose him. I love him too much. And he loves our baby and me just the same.

"What about him?"

"He's gone."

"Thanks mom," I say. I feel my body relax. I'm home and safe with Isaiah.

"It's not a problem," she says and hugs me.

Isaiah and I walk upstairs and I lead him to my room. It's exactly the way I left it. Clothes thrown on the floor and various items of mine laying, useless and tossed aside.

A few minutes later Carla peeks her head in and tells us she's gonna wash our clothes. We both nod and she leaves, closing the door behind her. I strip and get in the shower. Isaiah follows me and gets in the shower behind me. I have a very large shower. Although the one in Carla's room is bigger than mine.

Isaiah nips at my neck and hugs me from behind. "Not now Isaiah," I tell him. "I'm tired," I yawn. "We've been on the road for eight and a half days. We finally have a place to sleep. A permanent place to sleep." I turn to face him and put my arms around his neck. "Let's just shower and get some sleep."

He kisses me gently, "okay," he whispers.

We finish our shower and put on clothes Carla set in my room. I guess she found clean ones in our bags and set them in my room while we showered.

I stretch out on my bed and rub my belly. Isaiah lays next to me and puts his head on my chest and his left hand on my belly. I turn the TV in my room on and we start watching a movie. I see my door crack open and Carla smiles and shakes her head then closes my door.

Isaiah starts to snore a little. I giggle and then yawn. I close my eyes and soon I'm asleep.

Chapter 15

Where did he go? Why did he leave? Is it because he's afraid of his true feelings about me and the baby? Oh I wish he would talk to me about shit like this when it comes up. But instead he runs. He fucking runs from everything he can't express or face. I need to find him.

And quick! I have a horrible feeling about him leaving. Sheryl, leave to find him right now!

"Sheryl, where do you think he went?"

"I don't know," I snap at her. "If I knew I would be going to my car to find him. The only place he could go is out of Kentucky. He wouldn't risk going to Cliff Point because he knows Snake and everyone else is trying to find him. And kill him." I pace the living room floor, racking my brain for all possible places he could be.

Cliff Point. He's at Cliff Point! You know this! Go and get him!

"Why don't you wait here for a few minutes and see if he comes back? And if he does no worries," Carla explains. Her voice calm, she could care less if he comes back. Then she'll have it her way and I'll lose what matters most to me.

"No, I'm not just gonna sit here and wait for him to come back," I hiss at her. "I need to find him. I can't lose him!"

"Sweetie, if he wanted to stay with you he would have. But he didn't. He is an example of a dead beat guy. He's just like your father."

"Take it back!" I yell at her. "Isaiah is nothing Frank and never will be. Isaiah loves me and our baby. The only reason he would leave is to clear his head. I'm gonna go find him whether you like it or not," I hiss at her. I jog upstairs and grab my denim jacket and my car keys.

Carla grabs my arm as I reach for the door. "You leave this house to find him and you will not be allowed back," she sneers.

An empty threat. She'll always want you back home. Very true. She'll just beg for me to come back home.

"I thought you wanted me back Carla," I hiss back.

"I did, and still do but if you don't come back with him, don't bother coming back at all," she tells me. Her body gives away that she's lying.

"I'll find him, and when I do I'm gone."

Yeah! Stand up for yourself!

"Sheryl wait," she says. Her whole facial expression changes. It goes from angry to sympathetic. "Sit down a minute," she says. I sigh and follow her to the living room.

"I know you love him and I know he loves you. I see the way you two look at each other and the way you to act around each other. You're made for each other. I'm not gonna let you find him alone," she explains. "Know I want you to think, where would he go to clear his head?"

I sit back and think. Where would he go to clear his head and think? "Cliff Point," I murmur. "That's where he always went. Cliff Point is where we all go to think and clear our heads," I explain.

Get off the fucking couch and go! Something bad is happening!

"Then we're going to Cliff Point," Carla says.

Halleluiah!

"No, you're not. I am. It's too dangerous for you to go there," I explain to her.

Oh my God would you just go get him already?! I growl at my internal battle. Stop cutting in!

"Whether you like it or not, I am going with you to Cliff Point. I'll take my car, you take yours. I'll follow a safe distance behind you and then drive past the cliff when you pull in. that way it doesn't seem as if I came with you to find him. Nobody will suspect anything then. Now will they?"

Whoa, Carla just had a brilliant idea. What is she hiding? My internal battle shows a crooked grin and rests her chin in her hand.

"When did you become such a bad ass?" I ask her. One eye brow raised, what IS she hiding?

She just smiles. She turns her back to me and lifts up her shirt. A large tiger tattoo covers her back. How have I never seen that before?

"I used to go to Cliff Point all the time when I was your age," she explains. "My nick name was Slash," she adds. "I knew what the place was like when I went and I wanted to keep you from it. I did the same things you did growing up. But you going has made you a strong individual. I'm proud of you despite the fact you got knocked up," she explains.

We both laugh a little.

"Why Slash though?" I ask her. It's peeked my interest.

"I used to carry a knife. To protect myself. Cliff Point is sort of how I met Frank," she explains. "I would cut some people up. And that's how I got my nickname."

"Wow, and to think I thought you were just a bitch about not letting me go," I say and chuckle a little.

Carla smiles and laughs a little. She looks me dead in the face and gets serious, "Now, are we going or not?"

"Let's go," I tell her. She nods and grabs her car keys. I get in my car and start it. I look down at my belly and rub it, "let's go find daddy," I say.

I drive to the end of the driveway and turn onto the main road. Carla following a safe distance behind me. By now Isaiah is at Cliff Point, he had to walk the whole way so he's there by now. *Just get to him quick!*

It doesn't take long to walk there from Carla's house. I call Carla, "Hey I'm gonna drive slow when we get there see if I see him then pull in," I tell her.

"Okay sounds like a plan," she says. I hang up and slow down. The closer we get the more anxious I get. What if Snake found him and they're beating him until he dies? No don't think like that. None of them know we are here. Maybe it's still safe for him to be there.

I'm not so sure! Just hurry!

I turn my head to the left and see a huge crowd. Fuck, they've found him. My internal battle hides her face in her hands. Periodically looking through her fingers to see what's going on.

They know we're here. I park my car and turn it off as fast as I can. I run to where everyone is and push my way through them to get to Isaiah. "Stop it Snake! You're gonna kill him!" I yell as I scratch at him.

He stops punching Isaiah and rears back and hits me. I fall to the ground and clutch my face. Pain radiates from where he hit me. *He hit you!*

I hesitate as I stand back up and punch him back. He stumbles backwards and I run to Isaiah.

"Isaiah wake up, come on wake up," I beg him. His face is busted up and bleeding. One of his eyes already turning black. I see Snake rear back to hit one or both of us again and I throw my hands up at him. "Dammit Snake stop!" I yell at him.

"And why the fuck should I Claw? We told you he was bad news. You two don't need to be together. He's getting what he fucking deserves," Snake hiss's. "So tell me why the fuck should I stop?"

I look back at Isaiah and wipe the blood running down his cheek off. I look at my belly and then back up at Snake. "Because I'm pregnant," I tell him.

"What the fuck?" he yells. "You're lying," he says. The crowd backs up in shock. Gasps coming from all of them. It's very, very rare someone from Cliff Point gets pregnant. There's been a few uh oh's but they were just scares. This is real.

I hear Isaiah moan and watch him grab at his side. His face scrunches up in pain. "Sheryl, get...get out of here," he breathes.

"Not without you," I whisper as a tear falls down my cheek. "I'm not leaving you behind. I need you. Our baby needs you."

"But the baby...not safe...go," he breathes. His hand rubs my belly gently, leaving a few blood smears on my shirt.

"Snake I'm not lying," I say and pull my denim jacket off. I fold my jacket up and put it under Isaiah's head and set his head in my lap. "We'll be okay," I tell Isaiah. He looks up at me, pain in his eyes, and nods.

Oh my, I even love him. He can't die!

"When did that happen?" Snake growls.

"Almost four months ago," I tell him. I turn my attention back to Isaiah. His eyes have closed again. "Isaiah open your eyes and look at me," I demand. "I'm gonna get you help okay," I say as I start to cry. "I'm gonna get help," I whisper as my sobs start to consume me. "I love you and I need you. Stay with me please. Our baby needs you," I tell him.

"Isaiah doesn't love you," Snake says. "If he did he wouldn't have come here to risk himself getting hurt or killed. Now back the fuck away from him!"

"No Snake!" I yell back. I set Isaiah's head on the ground and stand up. I slap him and flick my nails against his cheek. Blood flows down his face and neck. "He came here to clear his head and you think he doesn't love me! If he didn't he wouldn't have slept with me and only me for the past year! He wouldn't have been there when I found out I was pregnant! And he wouldn't have run away with me! Leave him the fuck alone Snake!" I yell even louder.

Snake just stands there in shock. His mouth agape. "Close your fucking mouth, or I'll close it for ya," I hiss through clenched teeth. Hot tears roll down my face, my fists clenched at my sides, "If you think for one damn second that I will let you harm him anymore you are sadly mistaken Snake. I love him and he loves me. He loves our baby. Now stay the fuck away from him!

"I don't know why you think you have this need to protect me all the fucking time. I can care for myself. Isaiah takes care of me. He's been there for me more than you have. Now leave him the fuck alone. I don't want to see you ever again Snake. I'm done with you and this hell hole." Wolf comes in to view and he looks as if he understands my words and looks shameful. He drops his head and I point to him, "You."

I walk towards him and slap him. "You are awful in bed and should be ashamed of trying to kill my boyfriend. I'm done with you as well."

Yeah! Show them who's boss! I high five my internal battle. At least this time we agree on leaving this place behind.

It stays silent for a while when I hear what sounds like an ambulance in the distance. Thank The Lord I let Carla follow me. Everyone disperses and leaves as quickly as possible. Snake and Wolf stand in shock as I care for Isaiah.

The ambulance stops next to us and they put Isaiah on a stretcher. "Please let me go with him!" I yell at the EMT who's refusing to let me go with him.

"Are you family?" he asks me.

"I'm his girlfriend, he has no one else," I tell them. My tears starting anew as Isaiah moans and grabs at his side. Oh what did they do to him?

He sighs, "Fine, you can ride." I hop in the back of the ambulance and grab Isaiah's hand.

As the ambulance speeds down the road Carla texts me, "Following close behind the ambulance." I read it but let it alone.

A few minutes later Snake texts me, "Following in your car. I want to talk to you when we get there." I leave that message alone as well. All I care about is Isaiah.

I see Isaiah open his good eye and he looks at me. The EMT working on him shines a light in Isaiah's eyes and then checks other things. "Sheryl, I love you," he whispers. His hand squeezes mine and he smiles a small smile.

"I love you, too Isaiah," I whisper back as I start to cry. He grips me hand tighter as the EMT looks at the wound in his side.

"I'm sorry…sorry that I left," he breathes.

"It's okay, don't worry about that," I tell him. "I'm okay."

"Snake hit you," he says. He starts getting angry.

Oh Isaiah! He loves you so, and he wants to keep you safe even if he is severely hurt.

"I'm fine, I'll be okay," I reply.

"You sure?"

"Yes, the baby is fine too," I tell him.

He sighs, "thank goodness."

"Jake step on it! He's losing a lot of blood back here!" the EMT shouts.

"Isaiah," I gasp. "Isaiah stay with me please, don't leave me!" I holler.

"Ma'am please remain calm," he tells me. I give him my go-to-hell look and he ignores it. "Heart rate falling! Push ETA to ten minutes!"

"This is job number 2270, ETA ten minutes, code blue over," the driver says.

"Dispatch for job 2270 code blue, staff standing by," I hear a female voice say through his walkie talkie.

The ambulance stops soon after and they wheel Isaiah into the ER. Nurses and doctors come from all directions to tend to Isaiah. I try to stay with him but a male burse holds me back. "Ma'am you can't go back there, we'll come get you when they've finished working on him," he tells me. I try to fight his hold but he's too strong.

"Isaiah!" I holler. "Isaiah!"

"Ma'am please remain calm." I give up my struggle and go sit in the waiting room with my head in my hands and cry.

"Sheryl," I hear Carla say. I look up and she walks over to me. "What's going on?"

"I don't know," I tell her. "Snake wants to talk to me. About what I don't know," I tell her. "And I want to be with Isaiah. He started losing blood and they said his heart rate started falling." I start sobbing harder. Carla hugs me to her and about that time Snake walks over to me.

"We need to talk," he says quietly. I nod and follow him. I notice the huge bandage on his cheek from where I scratched him. He stops a few feet away from Carla. Just out of ear shot for her. "Look, I didn't realize you two were so madly in love. He tried explaining before we attacked him but I told him to shut it."

"Damn you Snake!" I yell and slap him. "Because you're so damn hard headed the father to my child is on the verge of death. You never listen to anyone. This is all your fault!" I yell at him. My tears stream down my face again.

Damn him! Make him leave!

"Look I'm sorry. I really am sorry. I should have listened to him before I beat the shit out of him. And I didn't. If it makes you feel any better I'll always be here if something does happen to him," he tells me.

"No Snake. I don't want anything to do with you anymore. You've hurt a part of me. And that part is laying on a table in the ER. I hate you for what you've done. I no longer call you or Wolf my brother," I tell him.

"Claw come on," he says.

"Don't call me that anymore. I'm done with Cliff Point. All of that is behind me," I tell him. "I told you that at Cliff Point."

"Sheryl, please. I'm sorry for all of this."

"No, go home Snake. Take Wolf with you," I tell him and turn back around. I sit next to Carla and start crying again. I hear two chairs move next to me and Snake and Wolf sit down.

I feel something strange in my belly and look at Carla concerned. "What?" she asks.

"It feels like something just crawled across my stomach," I tell her.

"The baby is kicking Sheryl," she tells me.

I smile and put a hand on my belly. I start to cry again. Isaiah missed it. "This is your fault," I snap at Snake. "Isaiah missed something great because of you."

"How many times do I have to say sorry?" he sighs and looks at me with exaggeration.

"Not enough," I tell him. "You'll never say it enough."

Not even for me to forgive him. Ass. I agree with my internal battle.

We sit there for what feels like an eternity until the ER doors open. "Are you Isaiah's family?" the doctor asks us all.

"I'm his girlfriend," I say. "I'm the only family he has."

"He's doing fine; we stitched up the stab wound in his side. He'll be just fine. He's awake and asking for you," the doctor says. "He does have stitches on his face and one of his eyes is black and swollen shut. So just be careful," he warns.

"Okay, thank you," I say. He tells me where Isaiah's room is and I practically run to his room.

I get to his room and open the door. He looks at me. "Isaiah," I say and start to cry. I run to him and wraps his arms around me in a huge embrace.

"Shh, hush. I'm alive, I'm okay," he whispers. I kiss him gently and he kisses back. I'm so glad he's alive.

He releases me and I get angry. "Why did you go there?" I snap at him. "Knowing they were after us. Especially you." I slap his leg out of anger.

"I'm sorry, that's where I always go to think. You of all people know that," he explains. "So don't get mad at me."

"Isaiah you have no idea how worried I've been. They could have killed you. They almost did. If it wasn't for me showing up you would have been killed," I tell him. I feel my tears start anew. "And then where would I be? Where would me and the baby be huh?" I murmur. "I can't imagine a world without you in it. I wouldn't know how to keep going."

Isaiah hugs me to him again. "I'm sorry; I wasn't thinking when I left. I'm alive though. Stop crying, everything is okay," he tells me.

I feel safe in his arms. They bring me comfort and make me feel home. They're so strong as he holds me to him. I love him so much. I didn't think it was possible to love him as much as I do. I would do anything for him and he would do the same for me. We are inseparable. An unbreakable force. Nothing can keep us apart. Absolutely nothing can.

I feel the baby kick again and I can't help but laugh and grin. "While you were in the ER you missed something," I tell him.

"What'd I miss?" he asks. A smile plays on his lips and eventually he smiles a broad smile that reaches his eyes.

"Baby's first kick," I tell him.

"Come here," he tells me. He slides over in his hospital bed and pats the empty spot. I lay next to him and he puts an arm around me and his other hand on my stomach. His thumb moves gently back and forth across my belly. He kisses my forehead and I smile. The baby kicks and he grins. "Well I'll be here for every kick after."

"Now that's what I want to hear," I smile and kiss him. Isaiah smiles and kisses me again.

Chapter 16

"Any chance we'll see Snake and Wolf again?" Isaiah asks me. He sits up in his hospital bed to eat his lunch.

"I don't know, I told him I didn't want to see him or Wolf again. And I sure as hell don't want to go back to Cliff Point," I say flatly.

Isaiah eats the rest of his lunch in silence. I just stare at him as he eats. His left eye swollen shut and black. Stitches across his cheek. He is still the most gorgeous human being in the world. He glances at me and winks with his good eye. I can't help but giggle and run my hand across my stomach.

The hospital door opens and Carla walks in. "Hey," she says with a smile. Me and Isaiah nod. He pushes his tray away and pats the bed next to him. I sit next to him and Carla takes the chair I was sitting in. "I looked at your chart Isaiah. Looks like you'll be going home soon. Tomorrow I do believe," she says.

I feel Isaiah's arms wrap around my waist and he smiles as he nuzzles my back. I wince a little from the bruise Snake left on my back. Isaiah doesn't seem to notice. He pats my belly and I grin at him.

"Good, I'm tired of this place," he grins. "I don't get any privacy. Every time I move someone comes rushing in here to see if I'm okay."

Oh Isaiah. My internal battle grins and shakes her head at him. Isaiah hates constant checkups.

"And it doesn't help that you make my heart rate monitor go up when you sashay to the bathroom in that way you have," he adds with a smirk. He pinches my ass and I yelp.

"Would you two stop," Carla smiles and laughs. "You two are so cute. But I'll leave you alone. Oh and Isaiah your doctor will be in soon to talk with you." Me and Isaiah nod and she leaves.

Isaiah pulls me back and leans his hospital bad back so I can lay with him. I lay my head on his shoulder and he wraps his arms around me. Every now and then he kisses my forehead and rubs my belly.

We sit in silence for a while when Isaiah starts laughing. "What's so funny?" I ask and grin up at him.

"Nothing," he replies with a chuckle. I glare at him and after a beat, he tells me. "This. All of this." He waves a hand in a circle to emphasize his point. "After all the trouble we've been through, we are still happy and together. We're like the invincible couple. Nothing will keep us apart. Ever." He stares at me with soft grey eyes. Full of love. He kisses me softly. When he pulls away he leans his forehead on mine. "I love you so, so much," he whispers. "And I want nothing more than to be with you and only you. With our child. Happy together."

"I love you so much, Isaiah," I whisper. I kiss him gently. "I'm always happy with you. Even through our troubling last few weeks." He grins and kisses me once more.

. . .

I help Isaiah out of my car when we get back to Carla's. She's at work and has already explained to Dr. Bates the situation has changed. I unlock the front door and help Isaiah inside. His eye is still swollen shut so it's hard for him to see. I sit him on the couch and he winces with pain. "You okay?" I ask. I don't want to hurt him more than he already is.

"Yeah," he says through gritted teeth. "My side is still tender."

"Sorry," I say. I go to walk away and Isaiah grabs me. "Isaiah, be careful," I laugh.

"Awe, who am I gonna hurt worse?" he asks. "Me or you?" he grins and kisses me.

Always thinking with his second brain, my internal battle shakes her head.

"I'm more worried about you," I say as he kisses my neck. "You can't stress your stab wound or it bleeds," I explain to him.

"Ugh always with the wound thing," he groans. "I'm fixed up. I'm just injured not dying. Give me a break."

"Isaiah you need to watch yourself. I don't want it getting worse because you can't control your sexual desires."

"But my sexual desire wants my beautiful girlfriend."

"Well your sexual desire is just gonna have to wait," I say and walk away from him. Making sure he can tell I'm teasing him on purpose. I see him put a pillow up to his face and he bites it and moans loudly. "Oh catching on I see?"

"Damn this," he says and gets up and kisses me harshly. My body responds and I moan into his mouth.

"Isaiah," I moan. "Just be careful," I tell him.

"When does Carla come home?"

"Not for another three hours," I tell him.

"Good," he says and picks me up and sets me on the couch. "Here will do," he growls.

Me and Isaiah are laying under a blanket on the couch. Me snuggled up as close as possible without hurting him. Carla should be home soon. Although the sight of both of us naked on the couch might set her off. She doesn't like the fact we have sex in her house. We've only done it twice since we've been here so I don't see why it bothers her.

Probably because it's her house and her rules. Teen agers having sex in her house is not on the rules to happen. I frown at her. Always being right.

"Carla won't like walking in to two teenagers naked on her couch," I say quietly. I yawn a little.

"Two sated, naked teenagers," Isaiah smirks and runs his hand up and down my spine.

"Isaiah," I laugh and slap his chest playfully.

"I'm just stating the obvious," he replies. I grin and get up and start putting my clothes on. I sit on the edge of the couch and Isaiah stops me. "Is this from Snake hitting you?" he asks me. I don't answer him. I don't want him angry at anyone and then have him even more injured trying to beat the shit out of Snake. "Sheryl, answer me." I still don't respond. "Is this from him hitting you?" he asks and goes to touch the bruise on my back and side. His voice is angry. I can't bear to look at him. Although the scorch of his eyes bore into me like I'm being stabbed with a knife.

"Don't touch it," I say and pull away from him. I don't know how he didn't see it earlier. "It still hurts."

"Is that from Snake hitting you?" he asks me again. I feel a tear roll down my cheek and nod my head.

"It's from where I hit the ground," I tell him. "He hit my face. Although my face isn't as bad."

"Why didn't you tell me this was there? I could have done something," he says angrily.

"And what? Go beat the shit out of Snake and injure yourself more than what you are now?" I scold him. "Not everything can be solved with violence Isaiah," I add. I pull my pants on and then my shirt.

"I'm gonna go upstairs and shower," I state and walk, more like stomp, upstairs.

I get in my room and peal my clothes off again. I hop in the shower and let the water run down my body. A burst of cold air hits me and I shiver. Isaiah wraps his arms around me. He kneels down and kisses my bruise gently. He stands back up and steps in front of me.

"I'm sorry," he tells me. "Don't be mad at me."

"For what? Even if I told you not to you would still go beat his ass anyway," I tell him. I cross my arms over my chest and scowl at him.

"And you know why?"

"Because nobody touches what's yours," I tell him.

"Exactly. And by touching you he technically touched two of my things," he tells me. "You and tiny tot here."

"Isaiah, not everything can be solved with violence."

He still has to learn that. Give him some time. He's used to fighting to make things right. Both of you need a little time to adjust to this.

"I know, that's why I'm not running through the front door to go to Snakes to beat his ass," he replies. "I realize that all I will ever need is you and only you. And tiny tot here. I've finally got something and someone that makes me happy. I've been searching all my life for that and I finally found it."

"And where is that?"

"Right here," he whispers and puts his hand over my heart and the other on my belly where the baby likes to kick. He kisses me gently and I smile. I put my arms under his and place my hands on his back. He pulls away and looks at me with soft gray eyes. The first time I've ever seen soft gray eyes on him. "And I never want this to change."

"And it never will," I reply softly. He grins and kisses me again.

We step out of the shower and get dressed. We walk downstairs hand in hand. Carla is standing in the kitchen cooking something. "You guys hungry?" she asks.

"Of course," I smile.

"You're always hungry," Isaiah teases.

"Yeah, well," I say and rub my belly.

Carla laughs and we sit down. "Oh and Snake and Wolf and their mother are coming over later. It's kinda like an apology for what happened the other day," Carla explains.

I see Isaiah's eyes go from the soft gray he's maintained to a molten gray color. "Isaiah," I warn him. He looks at me and I grip his hand tighter, "cool it."

"Fine," he says through gritted teeth. He gets up and walks upstairs. My angry boy. Perpetually angry, I'm afraid. Oh well. I love him and all his angry ways.

"He okay?" Carla asks me.

"He saw the bruise from where I fell after Snake hit me. He's been angry about it ever since," I tell her.

"Oh," she says.

"Yeah," I reply. "I'm gonna go check on him." Carla nods and I walk upstairs. I open my bedroom door and see Isaiah staring out the window. "Isaiah," I whisper and walk over to him. I wrap my arms around him and kiss his back between his shoulder blades.

"They're here," he says quietly. I see his grip on the ledge tighten.

"Calm down please. I'll be fine. The baby will be fine. It's just a bruise," I tell him. "Bruises go away."

He turns to look at me and the softness in his eyes returns when he looks at me. "Okay," he whispers. "Come on, let's go downstairs."

I nod and we walk downstairs. "Sheryl I'm so glad you're okay," Momma Jeanine says and hugs me. "And look at you, your glowing."

"Thanks Momma," I smile.

"Snake and Wolf told me you were pregnant but not this pregnant. How far?"

"Three and a half months," I tell her.

"Awe, and Isaiah," she says. "The next time ya wanna run off and knock her up let me know head of time."

"Momma it was my idea not his. I found out I was pregnant after we left and I was already eight weeks pregnant by then," I tell her.

"Still, I was worried sick about ya," she hugs me again and I wince as she touches the bruise on my side. "You okay?"

"Yeah, I'm fine," I lie.

"Sheryl, let me see," she says. I huff and lift my shirt up. She runs her hand along my bruise and I notice Isaiah get angry again. He turns his head away. "Snake you did this to her?"

"It was an accident," he replies. "I didn't mean to."

"Damn bro, you don't do that to a girl that's knocked up," Wolf says.

"I didn't fucking know when I hit her!" he shouts and looks angrily at his brother.

Isaiah walks over to me and grabs my hand and places the other one on my belly. Momma Jeanine steps back. "As long as I'm here it won't happen again," he threatens.

"Isaiah, what did I tell you?"

"I know, I'm calm," he whispers. Although he's anything but calm. I can feel his anger radiating off him like the heat of a fire.

Carla walks over and tells us dinner is ready and we all sit down at the table in the kitchen. Me next to Isaiah. Carla to my right, then Momma Jeanine, Wolf, and Snake. Isaiah glares at Snake the whole time. I nudge him every now and then to get him to stop.

"So, Jeannine…" I hear Carla start a conversation with Momma Jeannine. But other than that it's the only conversation at the table.

Snake tries to talk to me but I turn him away. I don't have the urge to talk to him. Not after what him and Wolf did to Isaiah. I hate them. Both of them. They could have killed Isaiah. And I would be left alone.

After we eat we all go outside and sit on the porch in the cool breeze. A shiver runs down my spine and Isaiah pulls me into his lap. Momma Jeanine and Carla stayed inside to clean up the kitchen. Me, Isaiah, Snake, and Wolf are on the porch.

"Hey, I really wanna apologize for not letting ya explain the other day," Snake says and rubs the back of his neck. "I didn't realize how much ya meant to each other. And seeing it now, I feel like shit for almost killin' ya."

"Snake you always jump to conclusions," Isaiah says. "I'm not always a bad guy. Especially to Sheryl, she is my whole world," he says and kisses me. I smile and lean my head on his shoulder.

"Well I'm sorry for doing what I did. And I'm sorry I hit ya, too Sheryl," he says. "If I'd have known you were knocked up I wouldn't have laid a hand on ya," he explains.

"Whether I'm pregnant or not shouldn't matter. You don't hit me. You know that," I hiss at him. "You never hit me. And know ya have the claw marks to prove you don't hit me."

"I'm sorry okay? How many times do I have to say it?"

"Not enough Snake, not enough," I reply. I shiver again and Isaiah hugs me closer to him.

"You cold?" he asks me.

"A little," I reply. "I'll take you inside." I nod and he stands with me in his arms. Snake opens the door and we all walk inside. Isaiah sits on the couch with me in his lap and pulls a blanket over us. I grin when I look at the blanket. We almost got caught under this blanket a few hours ago.

"What?" Isaiah asks me with a grin of his own.

"We almost got caught under this blanket a few hours ago," I tell him and giggle a little at the memory. Isaiah shakes his head and laughs at me. Snake and

Wolf give us a quizzical look. Snake goes to speak but is stopped by Momma Jeannine.

"Snake, Wolf time to go," Momma Jeanine says as she emerges from the kitchen.

"Aight," they say.

"See ya around," Snake says.

"See ya," Wolf hollers as he walks out of the door.

"If you need anything just call," Momma Jeanine tells me. I nod and smile a small smile. She smiles back and leaves.

Carla comes in the living room and sits on the edge of the coffee table. "How many cigarettes have you smoked in the last few days?" she asks me.

"None," I tell her. Which is the truth. I haven't really wanted one. I haven't thought about smoking one with all that's been going on. And I don't think Isaiah has smoked either.

"Really?" she asks me. I nod my head. "Good for you."

"Thanks," I reply. I yawn and Isaiah laughs a little.

"I'll take you to bed," he says and kisses my temple. I nod.

"Goodnight you two," Carla says as we walk upstairs.

"Night," me and Isaiah reply.

Isaiah lays me on my bed and lays next to me and pulls me to him. I grin as he kisses me gently. "Goodnight you two," he whispers. "I love you."

Awe! He is such an amazing boy! If only you had listened to me in the beginning and not waited all this out! I shrug her off and smile as I lay curled up in Isaiahs arms.

"Goodnight Isaiah, we love you, too," I whisper. He leans up and I turn my head and he plants a gentle kiss on my lips. He slides down the bed to my belly and kisses my belly. He lays his head on my chest and splays a hand on my belly. He rubs it gently and I start to fall asleep.

I hear Isaiah whisper to the baby ever so softly. "Daddy's here, I'll always be here." The baby kicks and he chuckles and kisses my belly. "Let mommy sleep," he whispers. "I'll keep you safe. Nothing will hurt you. Ever. I love you so much." And with that we both fall asleep.

Chapter 17

I wake up the next morning with Isaiah's head still on my chest and one of his hands still on my belly. He's snoring softly. I smile a little. The baby kicks and Isaiah stops snoring and whispers, "let mommy sleep." I laugh a little at his statement. He's probably done that all night. "Don't laugh at me," he says sleepily.

Awe! This makes me cry! Emotional, even my internal battle is emotional.

I run my fingers through his thick black hair and grin at him. "Have you done that all night?" I ask him.

"Every time the baby kicked," he replies. He sits up and kisses me gently. "Good morning."

"Good morning," I reply softly. Isaiah puts an arm around me and I snuggle up to him. "How's your side?" I ask.

"Still tender, doesn't hurt as much," he replies. "Does my eye still look swollen?"

"Not at all, it's still black but it'll be that way for a while."

"Figures as much," he says and rolls his eyes. "What about you? Let me see your bruise." I shake my head. I don't want him to see it because every time he does he gets angry. "Sheryl, let me see it," he demands. I huff and sit up and lift my shirt. I feel his fingers gently run across the main part of it. I flinch because it hurts so much. "Oh baby, are you sure you're okay?" he asks me. His voice full of concern.

"I'm fine, it'll just be sore for a while," I tell him.

"Okay," he huffs. "Well since the two of us are in some form of pain why don't we just lay here in bed all day? We could have some fun," he smirks and kisses me. "Or watch movies or sit in silence or shower together. The list is endless; relive your painful past or mine."

"Let's just lay here, I'm exhausted from the past few days events to be honest," I tell him. "And reliving my past is not on a list for discussion for a couple weeks until all this blows over."

"I can live with that," he replies with a smile. "Besides, we have a full future ahead of us. With tiny tot here, who knows what the future will bring." He eyes me speculatively.

Oh he has a secret! Pester him for information! No! I shake my head at her. I want him to want to tell me. I don't want to nag it out of him. *Ugh fine, have it your way,* she sighs at me. But I don't care. I don't listen to her anyway.

We remain quiet for a little while. Snake texts me saying he's always here if I need him. Which I don't. I have Isaiah. Carla comes up around ten-ish and asks us what we have planned for today.

"Nothing at all," I tell her. "We decided to lay in bed all day and chill. Since both of us have had a trying past couple months." She nods and a few moments later walks in with breakfast for us. Pancakes, eggs, and bacon. Why is she doing this? And a few hours later she brings us lunch. A full lunch, too. Turkey sandwiches for both of us, with chips and soda. What is making her be so nice right now?

She understands we want our distance from her. And that me and Isaiah just want to be alone. But I find it odd every time she leaves my room she has a goofy grin on her face.

"Isaiah, I want you to tell me something," I say breaking the eternal silence of our morning alone.

"And what would that be?"

"Why did you go to Cliff Point that day?"

He sighs and lays flat on my bed. He puts his hands behind his head and sighs again. "I went to clear my head. Like I always do. After we…after we made love I didn't know what to think. I had never felt so strong for a person until I met you. And when you told me what we had done and how much better it was than before I felt as if I was losing my touch or that you wouldn't like it and you would leave and I couldn't risk that because I love you so much. So I went to Cliff Point. Knowing Snake and Wolf and everyone else was there. I showed up and they all saw me and walked towards me."

"Isaiah stop."

"I tried explaining to them but nobody would listen to me. I told them I didn't want any trouble. I was just there to explain and think about things. But they all ignored me. Snake hit me first but I didn't fall. I hit him back, defending myself. Wolf came out of nowhere and stabbed me, that's when I fell."

"Isaiah stop," I repeat. *Make him stop! I don't want to hear this either. It's heartbreaking.* I'm trying, shut it!

"I couldn't get a word in before they started kicking me and hitting me. Snake picked me up off the ground and God was he angry. He said, *"If you ever fucking touch my baby sister again you'll regret it. That's if I let you live,"* and that's when my life flashed before my eyes. The thought of losing you or you losing me killed me in that instant. I thought about everything. My life and how shitty it was before I met you. How much you've changed me. It scared me."

"Please stop," I beg him. But he doesn't, he keeps going. *I can't bear to listen to this anymore. I'm gone.* And like that the internal battle leaves. And I feel better. If only I could get Isaiah to stop talking about this.

"Sheryl, I thought you weren't gonna find me. I was scared. For the first time in my life I was afraid of dying and afraid of losing you and the baby. I was afraid," he admits. I can see the fear in his eyes. "I've never been afraid of dying before. Ever. And the thought of leaving you and tiny tot made me afraid to die."

"Stop Isaiah!" I shout at him. "I don't want to hear anymore okay?" I look down at him and he looks up at me. We're both here. Both of us broken people that found our way to each other. "I'm constantly afraid I'm gonna lose you because you have no regard for your wellbeing. And hearing what Snake did to you hurts to hear. I don't want to know."

He sits up and wraps his arms around me. "I thought you wanted to know. I won't tell you anymore." I nod. "I'm sorry I didn't just talk to you about it. I should have but I needed to think. You know how I get."

"Yeah that hard ass head of yours is always in the way," I reply. "When are you gonna learn that despite what we've been through we are changing?"

"Good question, but a better question would be: what are you doing to me?"

"Giving you what you've needed. What you've missed in the past and always wanted," I reply.

He grins and rubs my belly. "And what would that be?" he asks making sure I know the answer myself.

"Love." He swallows hard. His eyes look terrified, but he doesn't say anything. "Isaiah you know that's what I was going to say. You know it's true. That is all you have been looking for your whole life. And you found it in me." He just stares at me. "Don't look so horrified," I tell him. "You have nothing to be afraid of. Ever. I'm not going anywhere. And neither is tiny tot. We're in this for the long haul. We always stick together. No secrets, no lies, only truth and trust."

"Sheryl, I love you," he whispers. I see his body relax, as if some unknown weight has been lifted off his shoulders. He looks happy, serene. He looks like Isaiah, my Isaiah. The boy I have fallen deeply in love with.

"I love you, too Isaiah," I whisper back.

"I don't ever want to lose you. Ever. For as long as I live. I've never had someone mean so much to me before. Until I met you. You have flipped my whole world upside down and I thank God you did. And I want to ask you something. Something I never thought I would ask a girl in a million years. But I don't want anyone else. I only want you," he explains. "And I know I don't have much to give and I know we've been through hell in the past eighteen almost nineteen years of our lives. And I know we've only been together a few months."

"A year, sexually," I add. "So technically we've been together a little more than a year."

"Okay fine, I know we've been together a year but I want to do this."

It gets quiet. Isaiah looks at me with gentle eyes. Both of us laying flat with our heads turned looking at each other. Even though he has stitches all over his face and his eye is black, I don't care. He is still the most beautiful human being I've ever layed eyes on. And to me he always will be.

"What is it you wanna do?" I whisper.

"Marry me," he whispers.

My mouth drops and I feel like I wanna cry. Did he really just…? And before I can even think twice, "Yes," I whisper back. He smiles and kisses me.

"Awe," I hear from my door. Carla walks through my door and has a huge smile plastered on her face. She sits on the edge of my side of the bed and hugs me. "I'm so happy," she tells me.

"What for?" I ask. And how did she know?

"Well one of the days Isaiah was in the hospital I went and checked on him. You were getting lunch for the two of you. He talked to me about how much he loves you and wants to care for you and the baby. Sheryl he is such a good man. Better than your father. He asked me if he could marry you. At first I said no but he started begging me." I think about Isaiah begging. It's strange to hear. "Sheryl he loves you so much, probably more than you will ever know. That's when I knew he was good for you. You're getting married," she explains.

"I never thought this would be happening to you. You're so young but it's your life. I never knew how much he loved you. And I want you to know that you have made the best decision for you. I love you, and despite what happened between me and Frank, I'm glad you have found who you are." I smile and hug her.

"Thank you mom, I love you, too," I say as I choke back a sob.

You have forgiven your mother! Praise the Lord. Halleluiah! Let's celebrate! I grin at my internal battle. She's never too far away. And never will be.

Carla releases me from her embrace and I turn to Isaiah. "I love you," I say and kiss him.

Isaiah pulls away first and grabs my left hand. He slips a small, simple diamond ring on my ring finger and smiles. "I love you so much more."

Epilogue

Two years later

Who are we? It's a simple question now. Before when I asked myself this, I couldn't have even begun to tell you. And now, with my husband by my side, I can tell you. Through our long journey of finding each other, Isaiah and I realized how broken we were. But being together, helping each other see the light, all we needed is to be understood.

"Chase, come to mommy," I smile at our two year old son. "Where's Daddy?" I ask him as I pick him up.

"Daddy wif Snake," he tells me.

"Let's go find him," I say and walk towards the house. Isaiah and I moved out of Carla's last year. Isaiah got a job shortly after he was all healed and saved every last pay check he got so he could buy us a nice home to live in.

As for the wedding of our dreams, it was a small get together in Carla's back yard two months after Chase was born. Everyone from Cliff Point was there. Snake walked me down the aisle believe it or not. He said it was to make up for what he did to Isaiah. And it did, I forgave him later that afternoon.

As the wedding goes, Carla planned it and it was very simple. I still had to wear a dress and Isaiah still had to wear a tux. My dress was simple, strapless and fitted. And Isaiah looked amazing in his tux.

Almost everyone from Cliff Point came to support us. And the couple that has been together for years, they decided it was time for them to tie the knot as well.

"Daddy!" Chase squeals when he sees Isaiah.

"Hey little man," Isaiah replies. I set Chase down and he runs to Isaiah. He picks Chase up and Chase laughs. "Come to help?" he asks him. Oh how I love seeing my two boys together. It makes me smile.

"Mommy wooking for you," he smiles. "Mommy won't let me help."

"Is she now?" he asks. "Alright, that's okay. Maybe next time." Chase giggles and Isaiah kisses his cheek.

"Yeah Daddy!" Chase exclaims. He is a very exclamatory child. But we love him with all our heart.

I walk over to them and kiss Isaiahs cheek. "Hello Mommy," Isaiah says.

"Hello Daddy, how's it comin' in here?" I ask.

"Good, Snake is finishing it up. Should be good as new to sell," Isaiah replies. My car is going up for sale. We both got new cars about a week ago and my car is too small for Chase's car seat and all his things that have to go with him. such as his toys and diaper bag.

"I will say Claw, ya kept her up nice," Snake says as he slams the hood shut.

"What did we say about that nickname around you know who?" I scold him.

"Woops, sorry," he says and holds his hands up in defense.

"Chase, grandma is inside, go find her," Isaiah says and opens the door for him to run inside.

I giggle as he runs inside. His black hair bouncing as he runs, and his chubby toddler legs trying to keep up with how fast he's running. Isaiah kisses me gently and picks me up. I wrap my legs around his waist and he sets me on the hood of the car. "When are we gonna have number two?" he asks me.

"Yeah," Snake says. "Chase doesn't need to be an only child. If I'm his Uncle then I think he needs to have a sister."

Isaiah and I laugh. We have talked about having another child. But Chase is only two. "Isaiah we've talked about this. I don't want our children that close in age."

"Sheryl, he's two not six months old," Isaiah retorts. "I think it's time for another baby. Chase is the right age, he'll be three in four months. He'll understand. And besides he wants a brother or sister. He talks about it all the time. And Snake has grown up since Chase was born," he adds to mess with Snake. We all laugh at his joke.

"Hey, that little dude is a lot of work. Props to you guys," he says. "Especially Claw for popping him out. That was horrible listening to you scream."

Isaiahs face blanches and I close my eyes at the memory.

. . .

Chase's birth was not easy. My pregnancy was and Dr. Bates said delivery should be easy. Little did we know, Chase did not want to come out at all. It was too late for a caesarian so I had no choice but to push him out. The pain was awful. Unbearable. Even though I had an epidural to numb me, I still felt it. Everyone in the waiting room could hear my screams. I was in labor for twenty-seven hours.

Dr. Bates had to cut me to make it easier for him to come out, and it still took three hours of pushing afterwards before he finally came into the world.

"Sheryl, come on, we just need one more push," Dr. Bates tells me.

Carla to my right, Isaiah to my left holding my hand. I'm crushing his hand. "Ah! Ouh!" I scream. "I can't do this, it hurts and I'm tired," I breathe as I lay back in the hospital bed.

"Come on baby, you can do this," Isaiah encourages me. "Bring our baby boy into this world."

"Isaiah I can't, I'm not strong enough," I whimper. I've never been in so much pain in my life. Ever. And I'm exhausted. I just want to sleep.

"No, baby you're the strongest person I know. You can do this," he tells me. He kisses my forehead gently. "Please, we wanna see our baby boy."

I nod my head and breathe. "Sheryl, his heart rate is falling, you need to push," Carla tells me.

I push as hard as I can. Oh gosh does it hurt. I feel like I'm gonna pass out from the pain. I feel a pop and Dr. Bates saying something but I can't make out what she's saying. My world is going fuzzy.

Isaiah moves from beside me and I see him hold our baby boy. Wrapped in blue, dark hair on his head. He's crying. He's okay. I smile.

"Look at our beautiful baby boy," Isaiah says with a smile. A tear falls down his cheek. "He's perfect."

I smile wider and close my eyes. I'm fading. "Isaiah you need to go," I hear.

"No! I wanna stay with her!" he shouts. "Sheryl I love you!" Then my word goes completely dark.

I wake up and close my eyes again. The hospital lights too bright to open my eyes completely. "Sheryl, how do you feel?" Dr. Bates asks me.

"Where's Isaiah? Where's my baby?" I ask her.

"Isaiah is in the waiting room, your baby is in the nursery. But before you can see them I need you to tell me how you feel?" she tells me.

"Like I just pushed Satan out of my crotch I wanna see my fiancé and my baby," I tell her.

I see Carla leave the room and Dr. Bates closes the door. "Sheryl, do you remember what happened after you pushed him out?" she asks me. I shake my head. "After I cut you, you lost a lot of blood. You passed out. Everything is fine, I've stitched you up. Your baby is healthy and so are you. Now, I want you to refrain from sexual activity for thirty days until you've healed. Okay?"

"Okay, okay fine," I say. "Can I see them please?" I snap at her. "I just want to see them. Please."

She nods and my door opens. Isaiah rushes to my side. "Oh Sheryl, I thought I lost you," he sobs. "He's so beautiful, Sheryl he is perfect," he tells me. He kisses me softly.

"Isaiah it's gonna take a lot more than a ten pound baby to take me from you," I tell him. Isaiah grins and they bring our baby boy over to me. I hold him in my arms and start to cry. "Chase Luke Wyatt," I whisper.

"Sheryl, I love you and him so much," Isaiah says and kisses me.

"And we love you Isaiah."

. . .

"Is that why you two are taking so long to have another child?" Momma Jeanine asks as she walks out with Chase in her arms.

"Kind of," I say. And it's true, after Chase's birth I'm worried it could happen again. And maybe next time I won't wake up.

"My boys can't even keep a girl and you're married. Take ya time honey," she tells me. "You made something of yourself. Take all the time ya need."

I nod my head. Chase reaches for Isaiah and Isaiah grabs him. We all walk back into the house and I go put Chase down for a nap.

The house is quiet. Chase asleep for the night and everyone gone home. Isaiah wraps his arms around me. I smile and laugh a little. He walks over to the doors that lead to the back yard and stares out of them. He is still so gorgeous to just look at.

We haven't been to Cliff Point since Snake nearly killed Isaiah. It's too painful to go back. Isaiah has a scar on his side from where Wolf stabbed him. It goes from his rib cage to about three inches down his side.

We've dropped my nickname, the only one who still calls me Claw is Snake. And not around Chase, he's too young to know about mine and Isaiah's life before him.

Isaiah stretches up and his shirt comes up showing the end of his scar. He looks over at me and grins. "Gawking at me are we?" he asks.

"You're my husband, I can do what I want, when I want," I remind him. He grins wider and shakes his head at me.

"Come on, I have something to show you," he tells me. He grabs my hand and leads me upstairs. "Since I didn't give you a birthday present, I figured I would give you this today." He walks into our room and over to the night stand on his side of the bed. "Come here," he grins and waves me over to him. I smile, intrigued at his giddiness. "Since the engagement ring you have now is so small, I got you this," he says and opens a velvet box.

"Isaiah," I gasp. My hands fly up to my mouth in shock. "It's so pretty, Isaiah how did you afford this?" I ask him.

"Your car, someone's already bought it. They paid a pretty penny for it. I put all but five percent of it in our main account and went and bought the ring with the five percent. Happy late Birthday," he smiles.

"Isaiah I love it," I smile. A single tear rolls down my cheek. Isaiah wipes it away and grabs my left hand. He removes my rings and slips the new engagement ring on my finger. It's so much bigger than the old one.

I wrap my arms around his neck and hug him. "Thank you," I whisper. "But the first ring was enough."

"Sheryl, I love you. I wanted to give you something more," he tells me.

"Isaiah you have," I tell him. "You've given me this home, our beautiful baby boy, the two new cars in the drive way, a life I love. Isaiah you give me more every day and I couldn't ask for anything better."

He smiles at me, "because you deserve it. We both do. I never wanted this life with anyone else but you. We can afford these things now. All of them. I want to give you everything you've ever dreamed of having. And I will not deny myself of giving you whatever you want. You are my heart and soul. Someone who has made me realize hatred does not get me anywhere. And that violence solves nothing. The world could end right now and I wouldn't care because I have you and our son." He smiles his full smile, and my heart melts. He only smiles for me and Chase.

I smile and kiss him, "Isaiah Chase Wyatt, you know the way to my heart. I love you so very much."

He pulls me to him and hugs me tightly. "With Chase, it's easy. With you I've gotta work for it," he teases. His hands move to my ass and he squeezes. "Always so firm," he winks.

"Well then," I wink and kiss him. "Oh wait, I have something to show you," I tell him.

"My birthdays not for another two months," he grins at me. Well in two months it wouldn't be a surprise.

I can't help but laugh. I reach into my jeans back pocket and produce a folded piece of paper. "You give me more every day Isaiah, now it's my turn," I tell him. He looks at me confused as I hand him the piece of paper. "Just open it," I smile at him.

He opens the piece of paper and reads it then smiles up at me. "IS this what I think it is?" he asks me.

"Mhmmm," I nod my head excitedly. "I'm pregnant."

Isaiah stands and picks me up and spins me around. He stops spinning and I kiss him gently. He sets me down and leans his forehead on mine and whispers, "and you give me more."

Printed in the United States
By Bookmasters